BEARLY BREATHING

....

EMERALD CITY SHIFTERS
BOOK ONE

ARIA CHASE

Demimonde Press
AUSTIN, TEXAS

Bearly Breathing / Aria Chase. -- 1st ed.
ISBN 978-1-947101-00-5

BEARLY BREATHING

An Heiress in Distress

Breanna Dawson hears wedding bells in her future. The curvy heiress is engaged to Silicon Valley billionaire William Keys, and her parents are certain the marriage of convenience is the answer to her family's humiliating money problems. Breanna would do almost anything to win her parents' approval, but the thought of spending the rest of her life with a cold, cruel man is too much to bear — even for a dutiful daughter like her. The closer she gets to saying "I do," the more suffocated she feels. In a moment of white-hot panic, her survival instinct flares, and she flees.

But her escape goes awry when she crashes her stolen car in the middle of a raging blizzard and wakes up half-dressed in a handsome stranger's bed. Trapped in the wilderness with no way to get home, Breanna *should* be afraid. So why is she so aroused by the tall, mysterious man who rescued her? A single look from his emerald green eyes makes her body hum with need. His sexy smile, his possessive touch, and his deep, rumbling voice flood her mind with fantasies and leave her aching to submit to his every desire.

A Bear Shifter Meets His Mate

Bear shifter Rafe Cabello just wants to be left alone. Balancing the needs of his inner bear with running a multi-million dollar company is hard enough without the distraction of a relationship. But when a voluptuous woman wrecks her car right in front of him, he can't turn away. He pulls the unconscious woman from the crash and carries her back to his cabin to patch her up. He has every intention of getting rid of her as soon as possible. But his bear has other ideas.

Every glimpse of her pouty lips makes him salivate with want. Every swish of her ample hips, every flutter of her lashes, every graze of her skin against his sets his body on fire. Rafe knows that if he acts on his growing attraction to Breanna, there's no going back. His bear insists she's their fated mate, and with every day that passes, it gets harder and harder to deny his animal's fierce desire.

A Secret Revealed

But before Rafe can give into the passion flaring between them, he has to reveal his secret. And that secret may just send his sweet, curvy mate running as fast as she can all the way back to civilization...

CONTENTS

It's so easy to get whisked away in the hubbub of friends, work and busy-ness, but we need to take the time to be still and become aware of ourselves.

The small things.

The fact that we're still breathing.

Our ability to move.

The presence of love around and in us.

Our strengths.

Our opportunities.

Our journeys.

– GRACE GEALY

ONE

The snow had definitely gotten heavier in the last hour. Breanna Dawson knew that driving up to Canada in December would mean traversing through snowy mountains, but for a girl who had lived her entire life in southern California, the journey was a bit more challenging than she had imagined it would be.

At first, it had been an enchanting experience. She had even pulled over at rest stop and gotten out of her little green hatchback to spin around in circles, catching snowflakes on her tongue. It was kind of silly, considering she had been on skiing vacations with her parents to such idyllic places as Vail, Colorado and the Matterhorn in Switzerland. Still, there was something touching and innocent about driving through a snowfall during her reckless flight from her fiancé.

Her enchantment had faded as the snow had deepened, falling from the sky heavily now. Breanna was nervous. Not only did she lack the driving skills to take on snow and ice, but she was also concerned about the amount of snow piling up on the roads. She was also concerned William might be following her, though she couldn't fathom that really happening.

He was such a cold man that he would likely shrug off the news of the broken engagement with the same emotion he would show for a downward turn in the stock market report.

No, she decided with the twitch of her lips. *He would greet the downturn with more visible panic than he would losing me as a fiancée.*

It wasn't as though he loved her, and she certainly didn't love him. Their tepid union had been forged by parental machinations and William's desire to marry into the old money and higher echelons of a southern California society couple. When he looked at her, she didn't see anything but his ambition. There was no passion in his eyes, and his kisses were cold as ice.

She couldn't blame him, she supposed. Not because she was curvy, with generous hips, a rounded butt, and nice breasts. No, it was simply because she didn't feel a spark for him either. As she'd examined the relationship on the three-day drive leading her toward Canada, she had found herself wondering how she had acquiesced to the arrangement to start with.

It came down to weakness. Or perhaps apathy. Either way, she had wanted to please her parents, a task which she should know by now was impossible. Nothing she had ever done had pleased them, including her prodigious music musical talent with the piano. When her stage fright had stifled her ability to perform and the music dried up, they had lost even the slightest hint of pride in her.

It stung. And even though she knew in her head that a twenty-four-year-old woman didn't need her parents' approval, it was still difficult for her heart to get by without it. So when her father had suggested the marriage as a way to bring a cash infusion into his company and add to William Keys's prestige, she reluctantly agreed.

As the snow continued falling, Breanna almost giggled, though it was a bitter sound rather than one of amusement. At first, she had assumed William would see her curvy frame and decide she wasn't the girl for him. That hadn't deterred him, and he had shown no signs of calling off the wedding. Like an automaton, she had gone along with the whole idea, but her anxiety had increased daily.

Three days ago, when she had fallen to her floor in the midst of a panic attack, unable to breathe with the weight of dread stifling her, she had known it was time to draw an end to the farce—something she should have done weeks ago, before invitations went out and preparations were well underway.

There was no way she could walk down the aisle in three weeks to be a Christmas bride. The thought of marrying William, of lying in bed with him and bearing his children, had left her physically ill. Just imagining sex with him had triggered another round of anxiety and gasping for breath. Her maid had found her, sitting with her until Breanna managed to finally calm down and breathe deeply. Lupita had offered a tissue, along with some unsolicited advice that had changed her life.

"It is wonderful to please your parents, Miss Dawson, but it is even more important to please yourself. If you do not want to marry Mr. Keys, you must tell him now."

Breanna had nodded, her inherent shyness keeping her from hugging the younger woman, though she had wanted to. Fearing Lupita's reaction, she'd held back, but had uttered a sincere thanks.

As soon as the maid left, she had packed her bags and taken the hatchback that was intended for the staff from the garage. Her parents were less likely to notice it was missing to start with, and she figured she had several days' head-start before anyone discovered her absence.

After all, there were no dress fittings scheduled for five more days, and that was about the only time she saw her mother. She had certainly not been offered much input into the wedding choices, but perhaps that was because her mother had realized Breanna didn't really care what color the napkins were, or which flowers appeared in the center-pieces. She had just wanted to grit her teeth, get through it, and pretend it wasn't happening.

Breanna had impressed herself with her strength when she had walked away, though she knew if she had a scrap of real courage, she would have stayed to face her parents and William directly. Instead, she had chosen the cowardly way of sending her ex-fiancé an email, and she had set an automatic email to go to her parents the night before the next dress fitting. Sure, they lived in the same house, but they might as well be a thousand miles apart for all the daily interaction they shared.

Now, less than two hundred miles from the Canadian border, in the middle of Nowheresville, Idaho, she was questioning her decision. Not the resolve to avoid marriage to William, but simply her vague plan to drive north to see if she could find her friend from college.

Grace had been her best friend for a long time, but they had drifted apart after graduation, both returning to their homes. She knew her friend lived in Calgary, but beyond that, she was clueless. With the potential of being stuck in a blizzard, and the possibility of freezing to death, Breanna realized just how impulsive and stupid this plan had been. At the very least, she should have taken a hotel room and spent some time tracking down Grace before she just fled blindly into terrain with which she was unfamiliar.

Up ahead, something caught her attention. Breanna tapped the brake pedal lightly, and the car started to slow. As she drew closer to the object near the edge of the road, she gasped and instinctively turned the wheel, though she wasn't even close to hitting the large bear.

Holy crap. She was in grizzly territory. Or maybe it was a black bear. She couldn't be sure, never having seen one in person and having gotten only a brief glimpse of the animal in question.

As she started to pull over to the side of the road to take a deep breath and regain control, the car hit an icy patch. Breanna whimpered as the steering wheel spun in her hand, and the car began to spin. The car turned almost three-quarters of a full circle, sending her off the road, and the passenger side careening into a large tree. The impact pushed the car away, and she sideswiped another tree before crumpling her hood into a final large trunk.

The airbag deployed to prevent her slamming into the windshield, but she still experienced a huge jolt through her body. As the car shuddered to a halt, her head slammed sideways into the window. Hot blood immediately flooded the area, pouring down her face.

Breanna cried out with genuine fear as she tried to lift her arm to see the damage. She couldn't move, because the door had crumpled around her. She was pinned in the car, and her head was bleeding profusely. Dizziness swept over her, and though she tried to fight the urge to close her eyes, she couldn't seem to resist.

Pain flared in her head, and she blinked her eyes in an attempt to fight back the urge to seek unconsciousness. A shrill scream escaped her at the sight of the large bear sprawling across the front of her car, standing on its hind legs and supporting itself against the car frame with its front legs.

It was a huge specimen, but with arresting green eyes the color of pine trees. She'd never seen anything like it, but it was amazing. It was also the last thing she saw before she surrendered to the wave of blackness sweeping over her.

T W O

Damn, it was cold. Rafe Cabello didn't like the winter much anyway, since it was more natural for his kind to hibernate away. That was impractical with a modern lifestyle, so he compromised by wintering in his cabin sheltered deep in the Coeur d'Alene Mountains. It was den-like and cozy, but his bear had been restless, so he'd gone for a run. Rafe had left his clothes folded neatly on the front step before transforming to his ursine side and loping through the woods.

The car had been unexpected, but he had been nowhere near it. The idiot driver had clearly overcompensated at the sight of him, and now the little hatchback was twisted into a tree.

He had the curmudgeonly urge to turn around and go back to his cabin, but surprisingly, his bear was urging him forward. He didn't know what had made that side of him so social or concerned with others, but he grudgingly surrendered and loped across the road to the site of the accident.

He couldn't see anything with the snow and angle of the car, so he walked around to the side, and then the front. Reluctantly, Rafe clambered to the top of the car, standing up to his full bear height. It was an uncomfortable position, but he maintained it by supporting his paws against the car's roof.

He drew in a ragged breath at his first glimpse of the woman behind the wheel. It was difficult to make out much of her with the airbag obscuring his vision, but the blood trailing down her face alarmed him.

Her eyes appeared closed, so he risked changing in front of her. In less than a second, he shed his ursine form and was back to a human male. He reached for the door and handle, grunting with the effort to open it. The metal had twisted with the impact, and though he was a strong man, he couldn't tear the distorted metal from the frame.

However, his bear was more than capable of doing so. Rafe went to the back of her vehicle, thankful the hatchback wasn't locked. There was a jumble of suitcases in the back, and he sorted through until he found something useful. He didn't know the bungee cord's original purpose, but he hoped it would work to help open the door. After closing the hatchback, he ran back to the door, shivering as the snow struck his bare skin. He didn't notice it too badly with his bear form, because of his thick layer of fur, but in just his skin, he was colder than hell.

He could only imagine how the driver was faring, so he made quick work of fastening the bungee cord around the handle several times. Then he shifted back to his bear, grasping the bungee cord between his teeth. As he pried at the door with his claws while tugging on the cord with all his strength, the creak of metal signaled he was accomplishing something. With another vigorous tug and an extra surge of effort, the door popped open, hanging oddly.

As quickly as possible, Rafe was once again human. He went to the car and knelt down to check the accident victim. There was no one else inside the car, for which he was grateful. The way the passenger door had slammed against the tree, whoever was on that side wouldn't have made it.

Fortunately, the door seemed to have done nothing more to the driver than rip a long abrasion down her arm and a small gash to her head. He decided to bind up her arm wound first, spending a moment foraging through her things in search of something to use as a makeshift bandage before settling for a plain white camisole. The cotton yielded easily to his tears, and it was absorbent when he wrapped it around the wound.

His unconscious patient whimpered as he tied off the strip of cloth, which he took as a good sign. He'd been half afraid she was deeply unconscious, judging by the amount of blood pouring down her face. However, he knew head wounds could bleed profusely, no matter how minor. This appeared to be on the moderate side. Peering at the wound, he decided to clean and bandage it once he got back to the cabin.

It took some maneuvering, but he was able to get her out of the car without brushing her lush body against the mangled metal that had been the door. When he stood up, she curved against him, sighing softly.

It was still cold as all hell, but he was suddenly hot on the inside. A raging erection rose between his legs, and where her mouth pressed against his neck as she breathed in and out, he swore the skin was on fire.

Mate.

His bear was responding eagerly to the woman in his arms. Clearly, the bear had decided this was a woman to mate with, and Rafe tried to find a way to reason with that side of himself as he broke into a run, headed back to his cabin.

He winced at the cold against his bare feet, wishing for his paws instead. Unfortunately, he couldn't carry an unconscious woman in his bear form. If she had been even moderately awake, he could have put her on his back and instructed her to hold on, but she was out. That was probably for the best, because he couldn't imagine a scenario where a complete stranger would be okay with him changing to a bear and giving her a ride.

His bear growled fiercely in the back of his mind, and he muttered something less than polite to shut it up. Yes, he was aware of how urgently the bear wanted to mark the woman as theirs, but Rafe still had a shred of common sense. The snow was doing its job and helping him control the mating frenzy his bear was trying to incite.

As he searched for a way to bring his bear in check, he couldn't help glancing down at the woman in his arms. She was soft and rounded in all the right places, with the kind of body a man could hold onto and sink into as he fucked her lustily. She could also accommodate his length and his height. It was impossible to be certain through her coat and jeans, but she seemed to have generous breasts and a soft tummy.

10

Thinking of his cock inside her made him roar with approval in concert with his bear's growl. Thoughts of why he shouldn't desire her, or trying to persuade his bear that she wasn't a suitable mate, fled from his mind the longer he held her. She belonged to them, though she didn't know it yet.

As he approached his cabin, ducking inside where a warm fire burned, he laid her down on the floor beside the fireplace before running outside to retrieve his clothes. In his head, his bear was demanding he take her, bite her, and mark her as theirs.

"Shut up," he said grumpily. "I feel it too, but now isn't the time. Control yourself."

With his surrender and admission he also wanted her, his bear side decided to quiet down, obviously satisfied with his acquiescence. Rafe was thankful for that as he returned to the house, slipping on his clothes in the kitchen before going to the living room to check over the woman who had crashed her car at the sight of a grizzly bear in the woods.

She had curled onto her side, facing the fire, and she appeared to be deeply asleep. This time, he knelt on the floor beside her, checking her pulse with a frown of concern. Thankfully, it was steady and strong under his hand.

He examined her head wound and again and saw that it had stopped bleeding altogether. He decided to leave it alone for now. He didn't want to disturb her any more than he had to.

They were too far from civilization to make it practical to get her to the hospital, especially in these circumstances. It had been a long time since his training as an Army medic, but he figured it would be safe enough to move her to a bed.

The only bed in the cabin.

His bed.

As he scooped her up off the floor and back into his arms, he realized his body was already familiar with the feel of hers. She seemed to settle right against him as though they had been made to fit together.

He groaned softly, his cock twitching against the zipper of his jeans, since he hadn't taken time for underwear. This was a special kind of torture. Striding down the hall, he elbowed open the door to the bedroom and laid her carefully on the bed. With only one in the small cabin, they would have to make do.

Fortunately, it was a king-size, because he liked to spread out. Occasionally, he even slept on the bed in bear form, though his bear usually preferred to be outdoors for naps. However, there was a lazy side to his inner bear, and they had spent many happy afternoons napping away the winter days tucked up in that bed.

Now, the bed was more tempting than ever with its newest addition, and he could easily imagine spending many happy days tucked up with her under the gray comforter. He didn't even know her name, or anything about her, but it took all his willpower not to join her on the mattress.

Instead, he rustled through his drawers until he found a flannel shirt that had shrank in the dryer. He thought it would fit her without swallowing her.

It was awkward to undress someone who was completely unresponsive, other than the occasional groan. It was particularly awkward when he knew the undressing would not be leading to the coupling his bear anticipated. Now wasn't the time to mate with her. She clearly needed healing and attention, and he reminded his bear of that when it gave him an impatient growl.

Finally, he had her out of the wet jacket and jeans before stripping off the sweater she wore underneath. He groaned at the sight of her breasts pressing against the black bra, threatening to spill over. He only allowed himself a brief glance, not wanting to violate her privacy, but the sight of her lush cleavage was enough to fuel his masturbatory fantasies for months to come. At least until he emerged from his winter cycle and returned to the city for spring.

The flannel fit, falling almost to her knees, but the sleeves were way too long. He folded them up before buttoning the shirt, careful to avoid the temptation of touching her breasts. He wasn't going to be *that* guy.

When she was out of her wet clothes, he tucked her under his blanket and started a fire in the bedroom fireplace. After assuring himself it was burning steadily, he left his own bedroom and went back to the living room. He couldn't allow himself to stay in the same room and be around that much temptation.

His bear was being a sulky bastard, muttering and groaning as though deprived of a favorite treat. Since Rafe was feeling particularly grumpy himself, and also as though he'd been denied his favorite treat, he couldn't be too upset with the ursine side of him being so bad-tempered. He sat, staring moodily into the fire, as he waited for his unresponsive houseguest to wake.

THREE

B reanna's head hurt worse than she could ever remember before. Even the couple of times in college when she partied late into the night, drinking far more than was wise, she had never had a headache like this the next morning. The pain came in waves, and each time she tried to open her eyes, it grew worse.

It took her a moment to figure out the reason having her eyes open was so painful. There was a light shining into them. Some sadistic jerk was doing his best to make her headache worse. "Leave me alone," she muttered, trying to swat at the hand appearing before her face. A second later, a face came into view.

She blinked, uncertain if she was hallucinating along with the headache. "Who are you?" She couldn't decide if her voice came out flirty or terrified. Or perhaps it was just sluggish and thick, because that was how her tongue felt. "Where am I?"

"Here in my cabin. You ran your car off the road, so I brought you here when I found you."

Thoughts were starting to become more cohesive, and abruptly she realized she could be in far more danger in this comfy bed near a roaring fire than she had been in the cold car twisted into a tree. She was out in the middle of nowhere, in some guy's cabin, and at his mercy. Just because he had rescued her from the wreck didn't mean he had good intentions.

Forcing open her eyes, she stared at the man who was either her rescuer or worst nightmare. God, he was gorgeous. With dark brown hair, a narrow beard and mustache, a chiseled face defining perfection, and a large frame, he was practically a CGI version of every girl's fantasy.

She blinked. CGI? That sounded wrong. Maybe he was a hallucination, if she was having side effects from a concussion. She vaguely remembered hitting her head anyway. At that reminder, the pain flared anew, making her gasp.

When her blue eyes clashed with his green ones, it didn't help her clarify whether or not she was actually experiencing the moment or just dreaming it. His eyes reminded her of the bear that had been on her car, the animal that had indirectly caused her accident when she had panicked. That bear had had the same eye color.

Slowly, she shook her head, wincing at the new flash of pain as she decided that was ridiculous. More likely, she had seen this man at some point when he had rescued her, and her swollen brain had incorporated his green eyes into the bear's face that she had seen earlier.

That made far more sense than the idea of a bear and a man having the same shade of eyes—especially since bears probably didn't have eye colors besides black or dark brown. She made a mental note to check that, along with determining if she had cell service out here, and her head throbbed again as though rejecting the thought of any mental endeavors.

With a small groan, she touched the side of her head, making her arm hurt with the movement. Looking down, she saw a long bandage wrapped around her forearm.

She met his gaze, giving him a tentative smile. "Thank you for rescuing me and patching me up." How she hoped he wasn't the serial killer-type, or the backwoods hermit-type, who intended to keep her as his kidnapped bride. Not only would that be terrifying, it would be disappointing as hell to learn someone as hot as he was could be a nut job.

He shrugged. "It was nothing. Are you in pain?"

She nodded without thinking, and then uttered a small cry as another sharp pain pierced her head at the slight motion. "Oh, yeah. You know that pain scale?" At his nod, she added, "On a scale of one to ten, I'm at about a thousand right now."

He gave her a small smile, which only made him sexier. "I think it's safe enough to give you some ibuprofen or Tylenol now. Which would you prefer?"

She blinked, trying to follow his words through the invisible cotton muzzling her brain's comprehension. "Um, ibuprofen?" She said it as more of a question, not entirely sure she was making the right choice. He had offered her selection of pain medicines, right? Apparently so, because he got up and returned shortly with a glass of water and four brown tablets.

She took them gratefully, and the water was pure heaven on her scratchy throat. She uttered a protest when he took it away before she could finish the rest of the glass.

"Don't put too much in your stomach just yet. You don't want to vomit."

She shuddered at the thought of throwing up in front of the stranger. She hated puking under any circumstances, but the idea of a hot guy seeing her that way made her cringe with embarrassment. Apparently her injuries weren't going to kill her, or she wouldn't be so worried about her appearance or the impression she made on this guy.

She settled back against the pillows, and he tucked her in carefully. It was only when she lifted her hand to move hair out of her face that she saw the flannel shirt and abruptly realized she no longer wore her own clothes. Her eyes widened, and she immediately did an internal scan of her body in search of pain or strangeness that shouldn't be there, like between her legs.

Fortunately, she appeared to be wearing her underwear under the flannel shirt. Inhaling without thought, she discovered the shirt smelled like him—a curious mix of the outdoors, including pine, slight muskiness that was strange, but not unappealing, and a hint of cinnamon.

"Who undressed me?" She didn't know if she wanted to hope for him having a wife in attendance, because that would mean at least a fellow woman had undressed her, but it would also mean he was involved with someone and off-limits.

She was startled at the thought. Of course he was involved with someone. A man like him didn't stay single unless there was something really wrong with him–mommy issues, inability to face grownup responsibility, or a potential serial killer.

She hoped it wasn't any of those problems, but that would bring her back to the assumption he was involved with someone. She sighed softly, bracing herself for disappointment and adding the reminder she wasn't his type anyway.

A hint of color appeared in his cheeks, but he smiled in an attempt to hide his discomfort, though it was still visible. "I'm sorry, but I couldn't leave you in wet clothes. I was afraid you'd get pneumonia, and there's no one else here. I swear I was a complete gentleman."

Some impish impulse seized her, and she gave him a wink. "That's too bad." Immediately, that temptress fled, and her shyness returned. Breanna closed her eyes again, feigning instant sleep until she heard the door close behind him a few minutes later.

Only then did she allow herself to relax and ease into the slumber that beckoned. What had gotten into her, flirting with him like that? She often had internal impulses to say or do outrageous things, but she never gave in to those impulses. It was far easier to remain aloof and disconnected than try to be the fun girl when she was always to the shy, serious one. There was just something about the guy who'd rescued her and…the guy whose name she had forgotten to request. That was silly of her, but she supposed she should cut herself some slack under the circumstances.

***

Her enigmatic rescuer finally allowed her out of bed the next day. Breanna felt better, though her head still ached. It was awkward walking around in the flannel shirt he had given her, though certainly preferable to parading around in her underwear. He was so much larger than her that none of his other clothes had a chance of fitting, which was a new experience for her. She kind of liked it, almost as much as she enjoyed the scent of him embedded within the flannel.

She also liked the way he looked across the breakfast table as he offered her sausage, biscuits, and gravy, with coffee and orange juice. However, she soon discovered she didn't like the reticence of her host. Being shy herself, she found it difficult to make small talk, and he certainly didn't help matters with monosyllabic answers to everything she asked.

"Well, do you live here all the time?" She had at least managed to ascertain he owned the cabin, though she didn't know why he'd been out on such a snowy night. If she'd had any sense, she wouldn't have been out on the road either.

He shook his head, finally managing to give her more than one word answer. "Not most of the time, no. I usually winter here in the cabin, but I have a life in the city as well."

She thought about asking which city, but decided not to press her luck. Rafe was clearly not the sharing type. At least she had discovered his name before they sat down for the late breakfast, so that brought the sum total of her knowledge of him to about ten facts.

What he lacked in conversation, he certainly made up for as eye candy, she conceded. Breanna rarely felt such an intense attraction to someone she had just met. To be honest, there hadn't been that many men in the past who had interested her in any way.

She wasn't frigid, but she had never really enjoyed dating, or the anxiety that went with it. It was awkward to be reserved and unconfident, so she had shied away from dating, for the most part. There had been a few young men who had managed to break through her reserve, but her longest relationship had been less than two months.

A pang shot through her as she remembered Derek Falco, with whom she'd share those two months. A twinge of longing swept through her, though it wasn't for the ex-boyfriend. That was back when she was still in Julliard, before her parents had grown frustrated with her inability to perform in front of crowds and had insisted on her transferring to a state university. That had been intended as a humiliation in itself, because no one in the Dawson family had attended anything but Ivy League universities for at least six generations.

So she didn't miss Derek so much as she missed feeling the music flow through her, and the easier life she'd had back then, when she was immersed in the notes and bonded with her piano. Before her musical talent had become yet another disappointment to her parents, since her fear of crowds interfered with their career plans for her.

"Are you okay?" He asked the question grudgingly, as if he didn't want to care, but did anyway.

She managed an overly bright smile. "I'm fine. I was just thinking about college." She didn't expound, and he didn't ask for further information, so the conversation soon died again. They finished their meal in silence, and she worked beside him in the kitchen to help clean up the mess with neither of them speaking. It was a surprisingly comfortable silence, considering their short acquaintance.

After they had finished, she glanced at the snow covering the ground, along with fat, fluffy flakes still falling from the sky. They were much slower than last night's downfall, but enough to make it a daunting task to find her way back to her car. The thought of trekking back in the thick snow made her nervous. Taking a deep breath, she asked, "Do you have a landline up here? My cell phone isn't working."

She had checked that before coming down, finding it still in the pocket of the pants he had removed and draped across the footboard so they could dry. Since they had still been damp, she was in the flannel shirt, but hoped to have dry clothing soon. They were necessary for her to be able to leave the cozy cabin—something she was strangely reluctant to do. Something about her host drew her to him, even though he was almost as quiet as her.

He shook his head. "No, I come here to…hibernate." There was a touch of amusement in his voice as he continued, "When I'm at the cabin, I want to be left alone. I don't have a landline, but I do have a cell phone. The service is usually pretty good, but I guess the weather is interfering. You should be able to get hold of your friends or family once the snowfall stops."

She shuddered, unable to hide her reaction. She could just imagine the earful her parents would deliver to her. It would be even worse if William answered the phone, and it seemed like he was constantly at their home since they had become engaged. She supposed if she had loved him and their union had been a normal one, she would have enjoyed his proximity.

As it was, she had gotten to the point of sending Lupita downstairs to see if William was around before she left her room. There was nothing inherently wrong with him, and he was always polite, but the sight of him was a reminder of what was coming and had been enough to put her on the verge of tears.

That had been before her massive panic attack, but she supposed with hindsight she had been working up to one for a while and had failed to recognize the signs. "That's okay. I just need a tow truck, or perhaps a car rental place." She tipped her head sideways, looking at him hopefully. "I don't suppose you have reliable internet up here?"

The side of his mouth quirked. "You'd suppose wrong, Breanna. I have to have a dedicated connection to keep in touch with the office, so if you need to use the computer to contact someone, I'll show you to my den."

She walked behind him over the deliberately rustic-looking flooring, though it was smooth as glass under her bare feet, and into a room that was the quintessential man-cave. There was oversized furniture, a billiard table and dartboard, a state-of-the-art computer, and a stereo system probably capable of reaching an entire auditorium of sports fans.

He sat down behind the large desk in the even larger leather chair, though it seemed to barely fit his frame. He was huge, both tall and broad, and she realized abruptly that he must have carried her at some point last night. No man had ever carried her before, and the thought sent a surge of heat shooting through her. She made a conscious effort to reject the voice whispering in the back of her mind that she was too heavy even for him to carry.

There were days when she really liked her body, with its lush curves, burnt-honey brown hair, and vivid blue eyes. Those were the days when she hadn't run in to her mother or any of her mother's friends, and when she had spent the day locked away in her room, composing music in her head. The other days, the days when she was forced to interact with the people in her parents' social circle, and those who were her so-called friends, were the days when her confidence faltered, and she questioned everything about herself again.

He tapped on the keyboard before he pushed away from the desk, waving his hand to indicate she should sit down in the large chair he'd just left. She brushed past him, their bodies colliding for the briefest of seconds, and dizziness swept over Breanna. Her heart rate accelerated, and she found it difficult to breathe.

In the short millisecond they had touched, her nipples responded by beading to hard points, and moisture dampened her panties. A fierce flush swept across her face, and she looked away from him, hiding behind the veil of her hair in an attempt to hide proof of her embarrassment—and arousal. "Thanks," she said, still not looking quite at him.

"Sure. Take all the time you need. I'll be around." He sounded gruff when he spoke, before striding from the room without looking back.

She feared she had upset or annoyed him in some way, but she couldn't figure out how. After a moment's contemplation, she shrugged. Whatever had put her host in that state, she likely had nothing to do with it.

Breanna sat down in the large chair, which made her feel like a kid again. She recalled days when she'd sneaked down to her father's home office to sit in his chair and wait for him, back when he had still been proud of her potential, before she grew up and fucked it all up by becoming shy and curvy instead of confident, beautiful, and able to display her prodigy-level musical talents. Her throat clogged with unexpected tears.

Clearing the lump away with a small cough, she focused her attention on the computer. She didn't bother to check her email or try to contact her parents or William. By now, they would either know she was gone or they wouldn't. If her parents had detected her absence, she didn't feel like reading electronic lectures about her actions.

Instead, she went on Facebook and sent Grace a message, saying that she didn't have access to a phone at the moment, and asked if Grace would be open to a visitor sometime soon. Then she began searching for a tow truck near where she estimated herself to be.

Coeur d'Alene was at least an hour to the northwest, and the two towing services that appeared closer didn't have websites. Without a working phone, that was a dead end, and she assumed Rafe was correct that she would be his guest until the snow stopped and the skies cleared again. She didn't know whether to dread that prospect or regard it with anticipation.

FOUR

Rafe barreled out into the snow, no clear destination in mind. All he knew was he had to get away from the temptation sitting in his office. When she had touched him, his bear had flared to life—especially when his nose had caught the aroma of her arousal.

Knowing she found him attractive and sexually responded to him had made it almost impossible to keep his bear in check. Even now, his ursine side was growling at him and urging him to turn back to the house. *Yes, I know we could have her in just a few minutes, but give her time. She's still recovering from her accident.*

Hoping his bear would listen to reason, or at least shut the hell up for a while so Rafe could remember she was still fragile, he went to the wood pile. He had enough logs split to last him most of the winter, but it was good exercise, and a way to take his focus off his houseguest.

Our mate, growled his bear in the back of his mind.

With an irritated growl of his own, Rafe stripped off his jacket and picked up the maul, rolling his eyes. That was nonsense, though he knew several bear-shifters who believed they would recognize their mate on sight—or scent. The human side of him regarded that with a healthy dose of skepticism, but his bear seemed to have endorsed the idea as soon as he smelled Breanna.

The spicy musk of her arousal lingered in his nose even now, making his cock hard, and his need for her all the more urgent. With a disgusted sigh that sounded almost like another growl, Rafe turned his attention to splitting wood. Soon, he had worked up a sweat and had stripped off his sweater and the flannel shirt underneath. In just jeans and work gloves, he used the maul to split the wood and try to break his focus on/obsession with Breanna Dawson.

***

When Rafe hadn't returned after more than an hour, Breanna grew curious, and perhaps a little alarmed. He was obviously familiar with the terrain in a way she wasn't, but what if he had gotten hurt out there? It wasn't snowing as heavily as last night, but with the continued downfall, another few inches seemed likely. If he'd passed out somewhere, and she didn't go looking for him, he might end up buried under a blanket of snow and freeze to death before he was found.

It was a far-fetched scenario, but once embedded firmly in her mind, she couldn't push the thought back. Feeling silly, she got up from the computer, leaving Facebook open in hopes she would return to find a reply from Grace.

Padding down the hall on bare feet, she entered the bedroom and realized suddenly that it was the only bedroom in the house, with the only bed. She clearly wasn't going anywhere tonight with snow still falling heavily and no tow truck available, so she guessed she would make do with the couch.

Briefly, the idea of sharing the large bed with Rafe popped into her mind, but she shook her head almost immediately. She wasn't brave enough to ask such a thing, and she couldn't imagine a world where a man like him would want a girl like her.

She wasn't being too hard on herself, just realistic. She was the kind of woman who attracted intelligent, geeky, or desperate men, not the linebacker type. Not that she knew if Rafe had ever played football, but he certainly had the build for it. He had the build for a lot of things, like lifting her up and holding her as they fucked hard against the wall.

Her eyes widened at the thought, and she blinked to clear the image from her mind. Where had that come from? She didn't usually indulge in such crude fantasies of men. Of course, she couldn't recall the last time she had been so attracted to a man, whether she had known him five minutes or five years. Perhaps she just needed to get laid.

If that was the case, she had to look elsewhere unless she wanted to be rejected. He would probably be kind about it, though she couldn't be certain with his hint of gruffness, but it would still be a stinging rejection, and she'd had enough of those to last her a lifetime.

With renewed resolve, she checked her jeans and decided though they were damp, they would work long enough to check on him. Her ballet flats were by the bed too, but they were completely impractical for going out in the snow. Staring at them, she realized they were one more thing he had stripped from her. She shivered at the thought, but not with disgust. Instead, it caused a dart of desire to shoot through her, and she wished she had a memory of the events.

As soon she'd dressed and shrugged on her faux fur coat, hanging neatly on the coat rack and completely dry, she picked out a pair of snow boots she found by the back door. A small giggle escaped her after she'd slipped them on and took a couple of steps. They flopped around ridiculously, making her feel like Bozo the Clown, but they'd have to do.

She tromped out of the house and down the porch. A thwacking sound caught her attention, and she shuffled her way through the snow, unused to such depths. It never snowed where she lived, and the few times she had visited places like Vail, she had worn skis or snowshoes.

More often, she was relegated to the lodge. After the first couple of attempts to teach her to ski had embarrassed her parents to no end, they had politely demanded she stay at the lodge. That had hurt deeply, but she couldn't deny she lacked their athletic prowess, so she made it easy on everyone by usually politely declining their tepid invitations to join them on their ski vacations.

Slowly, she plodded through the snow until she came around the side of the cabin and froze. The sight that greeted her made her gasp softly. He stood in front of her in profile, stripped down to nothing but jeans, snow boots, and work gloves. The sheen of sweat made his bronzed skin glimmer even without much sunlight filtering through the overcast sky. Every muscle was exquisitely detailed and so perfect that any artist would have wept with gratitude to be able to sculpt or paint him.

She longed to be able to kiss him or run her fingers over his smooth expanse of flesh. Her panties were soaking wet in no time, and she was embarrassed both by her arousal and her inability to look away.

Suddenly, he froze, lifting his head. In a peculiar fashion, he drew in a deep breath before his head turned and his gaze locked directly onto her. She shivered under the force of the intense expression. Was she imagining that dark hunger in his eyes? She didn't think so, but she was too timid to approach him to find out. Instead, she stayed where she was and nervously called out, "I just wanted to make sure you're okay. You've been gone a while."

"I'm fine." He swung the heavy maul and wedged it into the large stump he used for chopping. The lithe motion made her gasp, and a new wave of desire flooded through her. She'd never seen anything so magnificent in her life as this man doing something so simple as cutting wood. Breanna realized she was holding her breath as it left her in a ragged exhalation when he turned to walk toward her.

There was purposefulness in his posture, and the way he held himself revealed determination and perhaps something else—something a little feral or wild. A tinge of fear made her spine tingle, but that was obliterated when he reached her, his hands fastening around her arms as he pulled her close.

Before she had a chance to question his actions, or ask what he was doing, his mouth was over hers. He didn't kiss gently or sweetly. He marked and branded, kissing her thoroughly and deeply, as though determined to memorize every bit of her mouth.

After a second's hesitation, passion she had never known spread through her, and she was eagerly returning his kisses with the same intensity. She was feeling rather wild herself, and she shoved back the voice of reason trying to admonish her behavior. It sounded too much like Estelle Dawson, and she was in no mood to have her mother ruin this experience.

Breanna lost track of how long they stood in the snow, mouths devouring each other. At some point, he backed her against the wall of the cabin, and she was vaguely aware of the rustic logs pressing against her back through the fabric of her coat and his flannel shirt. It was a minor discomfort, and she was easily able to block it out when his hands roamed over her body.

He made short work of the zipper on her coat before attacking the buttons on his shirt she still wore with equal vigor. She was certain not all the buttons remained by the time the top was open to her waist, but she would worry about what to wear later.

Her own hands were busy roaming over his bare chest and back. He was hard and firm to the touch, but with supple skin that invited stroking. As her hand traced the arrow of hair leading down his naval, he growled low in his throat. It was a sexy sound, so she repeated the motion until he did it again.

He was rough and ferocious, but with a tender edge that gave her no fear. She hesitated for just a second when his hand slipped under the waistband of her pants and into her panties. The first touch of his finger against her clit did away with any uncertainty, and she arched against his hand. Rafe rolled her nubbin between his fingers, making her already-wet folds super slippery.

She ached to be filled and whimpered as she pressed against his hand. His fingers dipped lower in response, and he clearly realized what she wanted. A moment later, two of his large fingers surged inside her, but it wasn't enough. She needed more as she arched against his fingers, rubbing her clitoris against the palm of his hand in her search for relief.

She'd never been so wild and out-of-control in her life. When she had sex, she did it like a proper socialite—quietly, politely, and without vigor. This uncontrollable desire was exactly what had been missing in her life, and the epiphany broke over her at the same time as an orgasm consumed her. She'd never come with a partner before, probably because she'd been too inhibited and focused on how a lady should make love, not on how she wanted to fuck.

There was a new hint of wildness and desperation in Rafe as her juices flooded his fingers. She could sense he was moments from pinning her to the cabin wall, stripping off their clothes, and surging inside of her out here in the open, where anyone could see.

The idea should have shocked or outraged her, but instead, it only made her yearning that much more intense. "Rafe, take me now."

Abruptly, he stiffened. His mouth tore from hers, and his gaze was unfocused for a moment, reminding her of an undomesticated animal's. She wasn't afraid, but she was cautious when she pressed her palm into his chest. "Rafe?"

Without speaking to her, he spun away and tore off in a run into the forest. It was the strangest thing that ever happened to her, and she stared after him with mouth agape for a long moment.

Finally, the cold penetrated her clothes—or lack thereof with his shirt open to her waist and her jacket on the ground. She bent to pick up the coat and shrugged into it as she wandered back to the cabin, lost in gloomy thoughts.

She must have done something to turn him off, though she couldn't imagine what. Was it her invitation to take her? Did he not like aggressive women? She firmed her mouth at the thought. She wasn't normally the aggressive type, but if she felt like coming on strong, the guy she was with should be able to handle that. If not, he wasn't worthy of her time.

It was an empowering sentiment, and she clung to it as the afternoon waned and darkness fell. As she stared out the window, sipping a cup of coffee while she watched for the return of her almost-lover, she couldn't help a hint of melancholy overtaking her.

Though she barely knew Rafe, their intense moment outside had felt right on more levels than she could have imagined. They had clicked right away, with shared passion of the same intensity, and he'd given her that orgasm in record time. She'd never had that connection with another man before, and she missed him. It was silly to be pining for someone she'd only known for a couple of days, and who wasn't a sparkling conversationalist who allowed her to get to know him easily.

For some reason, though, none of that mattered when she was with him. She felt comfortable around him in a way she never had with anyone, friend or lover, before. It was as though she had known him all her life, and he was the missing piece of her.

Staring out into the darkness, she sighed softly. Clearly, Rafe didn't feel the same way.

***

Rafe didn't allow himself to return to the cabin until he and his bear had reached an understanding. They couldn't pounce on their mate like that. She barely knew him, and she was probably freaking out by how aggressive he had gotten. Unfortunately, he hadn't been able to control the urge to kiss and touch her as soon as his nose detected the scent of her raging arousal.

At least he knew she hadn't been unwilling, though she had probably been surprised by the intensity of his embrace. It was only when she had spoken that the human side of him regained the upper hand, urging caution and a slower approach. He didn't want to frighten away his mate before he could claim her completely. It had to be her choice, and she had to know everything before he could in good conscience take her and mark her as his.

And he knew if he was inside her, there was no way he'd be able to resist the small love bite that would put his scent on her, marking her and warding off other male bear-shifters. Of course the pheromones wouldn't last, unless he regularly had sex with her and nipped her to renew his pheromone marker. That was part of mating, and an essential part with a human mate, who could be quite fragile to the passions of a bear-shifter.

His mark would protect her from other bear-shifters, but he couldn't protect her from himself if he went back to the cabin without full control. At some point in his wandering, he had come across her car again. In a conciliatory gesture, he had packed all of her things that he could fit into a large suitcase and carried it in his mouth. Now, as he neared the cabin, he paused where he'd left his clothes and transformed back to his human shape before dressing. The sharp chill in the air made him shiver in just jeans and boots, and he hurried the last hundred yards to the cabin, heavy suitcase in hand.

She was in the kitchen when he opened the door, her gaze searching the night. He didn't think he imagined the hint of wistfulness in her expression, nor the slump of defeat rounding her shoulders. It was obvious he had hurt her with his flight, and he had to explain his actions, to make it right. Somehow.

When she turned to face him, her eyes brightened for just a second, and the happiness in her expression took his breath away. A moment later, that pleasure faded, overshadowed by a cool distance in her attempt to remain aloof. It failed miserably, though he wouldn't tell her that. Instead of seeming withdrawn, she looked more vulnerable than ever, and he knew she had been hurt by others before him.

"Would you like some coffee? There's still half a pot." Her voice sounded relatively calm, but there was a hint of shakiness underneath.

She was nervous or upset. Even with his heightened sense of smell to analyze the pheromones pouring off her, his bear couldn't decide which. He put her suitcase on the floor and walked over to the coffeemaker. "I brought your things." After pouring himself a cup, he turned back to her. "Most of them, anyway. I shoved what I could in this large case. I couldn't carry them all."

His bear could manage the load easily, but someone would have to stack it on his back, and he wasn't a pack animal. The idea of transporting cargo for humans was repellent. However, he would happily carry her anywhere she wanted to go, starting with his bed.

Now, growled his bear in the back of his head. Rafe did his best to block out the ursine voice demanding they claim their mate. *Soon*, he whispered in his mind, attempting to sound soothing. He hoped that was the truth. If she could accept him, all of him, he would claim her, but not until she knew the truth.

"Thank you." Her voice was stilted, and she moved jerkily toward the bag. As she bent to pick it up, he intercepted her hand and lifted the heavy case for her again. Her eyes widened when he wouldn't release his hold on her as he took her back to the bedroom, setting the case on the trunk in front of the footboard.

Only then did he turn to face her, ensuring her gaze locked with his. He didn't release her hand, but he wasn't forcing her to stand with him. He could sense her hesitation, but she wasn't running for the door. "I'm sorry about earlier. I came on way too fast and too strong."

Her sweet pink tongue flicked out of her mouth to run across her lower lip, and he barely bit back a growl at the sight. His bear demanded he taste her, and he had to wrestle with the urge for a long moment before he had it in check again.

"It's okay. It was probably just a moment of madness or something."

No, he wasn't going to let her get off that easily. Rafe shook his head, bringing his hand up to hold her chin when she would have looked away. "No, it wasn't that at all. Actually, I suppose there was a hint of madness to it, but as soon as I smelled your arousal and realized how badly you wanted me, my desire came to the forefront. I couldn't control the urge to touch and taste you. I barely managed to stop myself from pinning you to the house and fucking you like crazy."

She gasped softly, but her expression didn't betray fear. Instead, her eyes darkened, and he thought he read hope in her expression. "You really wanted me that badly?"

At his affirmative nod, she licked her lip again, provoking a growl from him. Her eyes widened at the sound, but she still didn't seem afraid. Now, she was clearly on the edge of excitement. A deep inhalation confirmed his suspicion, and he could sense she was aroused.

"Why didn't you?" It seemed to have cost her great effort to utter the question, and she tried to look away again as her cheeks burned scarlet.

"I didn't because you're special to me, Breanna. I know we haven't been together here for long, but I feel like I've known you forever." Ignoring his bear's insistence that he reveal Breanna was their mate, he attempted a more human and rational approach. "Maybe it's crazy, but there seems to be a connection between us, one that invites deeper intimacy than one would expect between strangers."

Her eyes sparkled, and she nodded eagerly. "I feel the same way. I know we haven't spoken much, but from the moment I was aware after waking up, and I saw you, I wanted you." It seemed impossible, but her cheeks got even redder.

He found her shyness adorable, especially her ability to conquer it, though it seemed to cost her a great deal of personal strength. Before he could stop himself, he uttered the words that made his bear hum with satisfaction. "I recognized you as my mate the moment I smelled you."

Confusion clouded her face, along with her first hint of uncertainty. Before she could start doubting his sanity, Rafe held up a hand. "I'm different from anyone you've met before, I'd wager."

She nodded again. "You're certainly different from anyone I've ever met, Rafe."

"There's a world that you aren't aware of, just like most humans. An entire race of people, a hybrid species, if you will." He was mucking this up badly.

She frowned, looking upset. "Let's talk about this later. Right now, there are certain things I'd rather do to you. With you." Her face was bright enough now to lead Santa's sleigh, and he admired that she was fighting through her doubt about him to embrace her desire.

Still, he couldn't take her in good conscience without revealing everything. "I have to tell you something first. I'm one of those people, Breanna, and I need you to know that and accept it before I claim you as my mate."

After ensuring her eyes were on him, Rafe shed his clothing. She started to do the same, but he captured her hands in one of his for a second. "Hold off for a minute. Make sure you're okay with everything, and you know what you're getting into first."

Her gaze darted to the door, and he realized she was contemplating walking out on him. His bear roared his displeasure at the thought, and Rafe couldn't hold back the transformation a second longer. His bear took over, surging to the forefront, and he shifted in front of his mate, praying as he did so that she could accept him.

FIVE

Lord, he was too good to be true, just as she had feared. Apparently, her instincts making her feel that she knew him better than she did had failed her once again. She didn't know what he was talking about, but he was rambling on about hybrid species when all she wanted to do was lose her clothes and jump into his bed.

If he said much more, she was going to have to deny her desire and embrace her discomfort with his words. As it stood, she could at least pretend he was normal until they were done having sex, but if he persisted, that would be the end of this tryst.

Abruptly, Breanna gasped and reared back as a huge bear materialized in front of her. Holy crap. She blinked several times, certain she'd had a relapse of a concussion that had somehow triggered a hallucination. It was only when the bear laid down on the floor, rolling onto its back to expose its belly, that she stopped blinking.

Her gaze met the bear's intelligent green eyes, and she gasped again. They were the same eyes looking out from Rafe's face, and the same pair she'd seen on the bear the night of her car accident.

She couldn't truly believe the bear was a visual side effect of a concussion, and hesitantly, she reached out to touch the thick brown fur of the bear submitting before her. It was silky soft, with just a slight roughness that suggested wildness.

Without quite believing it, she sank to the floor on her knees and began rubbing the belly of the bear. Aside from being about a thousand times larger, and not dressed in goofy outfits, he was oddly like the dogs her parents had kept over the years, and she giggled at the thought of this huge animal curling up on her lap as she petted his ears.

A second later, Rafe was himself again. Her hand remained on his stomach, just a few inches above his cock, which was straight and hard just for her.

Her gaze darted to his face, and the uncertainty in his expression made her chest ache for a moment. He looked so vulnerable, but it wasn't his posture suggesting vulnerability so much as the openness of his expression, tinged with a hint of anticipation. It didn't appear to be happy anticipation, but rather one of dread, as though bracing himself for disappointment. Clearly, Rafe expected her to reject him and run screaming from the cabin.

It was the safe, sane, and rational response to what she had just seen. If she had a scrap of common sense, she'd already be fleeing into the snow and trying to convince herself she'd just imagined all this. Instead, she licked her lips and asked an asinine question. "Does it hurt when you change?"

The uncertainty eased slightly from his expression, though he still appeared vulnerable. "No, not at all. It's just part of who I am."

"You can control it then? I mean, you can shift whenever you want? It's not like werewolves, where they need a full moon?" What was with all the stupid questions? Shouldn't she be trying to find out how he had gotten into this situation, or better yet, requesting he take her to the nearest city as soon as possible? Perhaps she was still in shock, or maybe she was seizing an impossible chance to find out the answers to improbable questions. No, that couldn't be it. No way was she together enough at the moment to really be approaching this with a scientific outlook.

His lips quirked to form a genuine smile of amusement. "Actually, wolf-shifters don't need the moon either. For some, they feel the call more strongly during a full moon phase, and I hear it's easier for them to shift, but like bear-shifters, they control their form."

She blinked, for some reason finding it impossible to believe there were people in the world who could transform to animals, though her brain was rapidly accepting the idea that Rafe could turn from bear to human and back again at will. "Are there more like you?"

"Bear-shifters or shifters in general?"

Breanna shrugged. "Both, I suppose."

He nodded. "Yes, there are. There are several bear-shifters, including my family, that I know personally in the Pacific Northwest and here in Idaho. I also know several animal-shifters of various types. Of course I don't know them all. It's not like we have a registry, or we all get together for tea and Girl Scout cookies to discuss the issues related to being transmorphic."

For some reason, the thought of Rafe sitting around drinking tea and eating Thin Mints in his bear form, surrounded by wolves and all manner of animals, made her giggle. "This should be completely impossible." She made that obvious statement as soon as the giggles had faded.

He shrugged again. "Not really. It's simply a genetic divergence along evolutionary lines."

She arched a brow. "Why aren't there more of you then? I mean enough for the world to notice?"

"The population of shifters is much smaller than humans due to several factors. For one thing, our groups tend to band together to avoid shunning and dangers from humans who didn't and don't understand our type, so a lot live in rural communities and remote enclaves. We lost quite a few of our groups to ignorant humans in the past, particularly during the Dark Ages. Unfortunately, banding together limited the gene pool, and fertility is sometimes questionable in latter generations."

"I see." She licked her lips, wondering if she truly did see. If she hadn't witnessed the transformation for herself, she would have dismissed his words as mental illness. As it stood, she couldn't deny what she had witnessed, and she analyzed her feelings to determine her response. There was fear along with anxiety, but overwhelmingly, there was just pure lust, tempered with more tender emotions. She still wanted Rafe as much she had before, bear-shifter thing be damned.

"What did you mean when you called me your mate?" She wanted to hope it meant something besides a one-night fling, even as she acknowledged the complexity of entering a relationship with someone who could shift into a bear.

"Just what it sounds like. Several shifters from all the races believe we'll recognize our mates at first sight...or smell, as the case may be. Our sense of smell will always find our mate, supposedly. His or her scent will be almost overpowering, they say." He shrugged. "It appears to be true."

"I stink in a certain way to tell you I'm yours?" She didn't know whether to laugh or be offended.

"No, of course not. You smell divine. Somehow, my sense of smell is attuned more keenly to you. The nose knows." He winked.

Breanna shook her head, unable to believe what she was hearing even after seeing him shift.

"The belief has superstitious roots—that the gods had orchestrated it to be so, to make our lives easier and compensate for the hardships of shifter duality. The newer theory is we recognize pheromones that are ideally suited as a match to our own. Maybe it's a combination of both superstition and science."

He shrugged. "In all honestly, I didn't really believe it would or could happen until I met you. All it took was one sniff to know you're my mate. My bear recognized it right away, though I fought him a little bit to start with. It just sounded crazy."

Rafe closed his eyes for a second before opening them again, looking like he was bracing himself for battle. "I know it all sounds crazy, but the simple truth is you're meant to be my mate. You have to know everything before I claim you and mark you as mine. It wouldn't be fair to you otherwise."

Her brow furrowed. "Mark me? What does that mean? Are you going to turn me into a bear-shifter?"

He looked slightly annoyed. "Of course not. If you bit me, would I become only human?"

"No?" she asked tentatively, and he nodded with apparent satisfaction.

"Right. It doesn't work that way. You were born *Homo sapien*, and I was born *Ursus sapien*. You can't get infected with one or the other, and no one can change between the two. I am what I am, and I hope you'll be okay with that." He closed his eyes, looking like he was in pain. "I sincerely hope you'll be okay with that, because it's taking all my control not to mate with you right now."

"If I say no, your bear will just let me walk away?" God, that sounded insane, but it was a sincere question. She had to know if she was safe and could still make her own choices.

There'd been enough people trying to control her life over the years, and she wasn't going to accept it from her mate. The word should have been jarring, but it resonated with her on a deeper level, and she knew right then she had already surrendered to the pull between them, no matter what answer Rafe gave her.

His eyes widened. "Of course we will. It will be hard for us to let you go, especially since bears mate for life, and I'm unlikely to ever meet another match your equal, but I would never hold you against your will or force you to accept something you don't want."

Her smile broke free spontaneously, and she reached out to stroke her hand down his hard shaft. "It's a good thing I'm quite willing then, isn't it?"

With a suddenness that made her head spin, Rafe issued a growl and flipped their positions so she was underneath him. He was clearly surrendering to his bear side to dominate her, but in a sexy way she couldn't object to as his hands tore frantically at her clothing, literally ripping some of it from her body in his haste.

Even as he removed her clothes, his fingernails turning briefly the claws to rip the resisting fabric, he was careful not to hurt her. Not even the tip of his claws grazed her skin, and she felt no fear in the face of his desperate wildness. In fact, it stoked her own, and she spread her thighs wide once her clothes were off, ready for him to take her right then.

Apparently, her mate had other ideas. Instead of his cock filling her, his head dipped between her legs, and his tongue surged inside her wet slit. She cried out as he licked her frantically, his tongue rough but also gentle. It was a strange juxtaposition of sensations, to have him devouring her while treating her as though she was the most precious thing in the world to him, and she might shatter at the slightest roughness.

She'd never made love like this before. Men had tasted her, of course, but none of them had done so in such an intense way that made her feel so desired and needed that her heart cried out with equal fervor for him.

As his tongue swirled around her clit, two of his fingers surged inside her again, and she accepted them easily, already accommodated to their girth, but still longing for all of him. The size of his cock was intimidating, but not so much that she was afraid to try taking it.

When he flicked the tip of his tongue lightly under the hood of her clitoris, her world dissolved, and she cried out as a climax swept through her. She was still shaking and convulsing, her sheath contracting with the force of her release, when Rafe moved between her legs.

The head of his cock sought out her opening, and he surged inside her with an animalistic growl that raised the hairs on the back of her neck and sent shivers of excitement racing down her spine. She embraced her lover, wrapping her arms and legs around him as he sank into her.

There was a brief instant of resistance as her tight sheath adjusted to his large erection, and then he was fully seated inside her. For a long moment, they stared at each other, just lost in the bliss of being one.

Slowly he began to move, and she matched his pace. Unlike when he'd used his frantic mouth greedily on her folds, he made love to her slowly and tenderly, as though in no rush. She was thankful for that, enjoying the connection even as she felt the compulsion to crash against him to increase the rhythm. Their thrusts naturally sped up, and they pressed hard together, seeking release without ever wanting to let go of each other.

Rafe twined her fingers in his, holding her arms above her head, the backs of her hands pressed into the soft carpet. The lower half of his body arched against hers with rhythmic thrusts that sent spirals of pleasure shooting throughout her.

Suddenly, Rafe issued a sound eerily like his bear counterpart as his cock hardened further before it twitched inside her. Seconds later, his release painted her insides and triggered her own.

As the wave of her orgasm crested, he bent his head, and his teeth raked across her shoulder. Instead of tempering her ecstasy, the flash of discomfort only fueled her pleasure, increasing the intensity of her orgasm as she shook and shuddered underneath him.

It was only several moments later, when she came down from the emotional high of sexual release, that she curled against him and remembered his bite. "When you bit me at the end, was that the marking thing you were talking about?"

He nodded. "Yes. That marks you with my phero-mones and lets other male bear-shifters know you've been claimed as my mate. It will protect you, and it's also some pure macho bullshit that goes back to ancient days of terri-torialism." He grinned and winked. "Bears occasionally share their mates, usually due to lack of females, but bear-shifters aren't generally so open to the idea. When it comes to our mates, we're possessive and don't usually like to share."

She arched brow, intrigued by the idea of a bear mé-nage. "Polyamory is accepted in your culture?"

He laughed. "My culture is basically the same as yours, sweetheart, with just a few more complexities. But, yes, it's okay for triads or more to be *out* among bear-shifter communities, though as I said, it's relatively rare. Usually, it's confined to just brothers or very close friends who share a woman."

"How does that work with babies? Do they know who the father is?" Suddenly, Breanna groaned. "Oh no."

"What?" He had stiffened, the hair on his body bris-tling as though he was preparing for attack. "What's wrong?"

She shook her head. "It's just that I'm not using any birth control, and you definitely didn't either."

His eyes sparkled, and he sounded gruff, but lovable, when he said, "Nothing would make me happier than to see you round with my cubs, even though it's early in the relationship." He closed his eyes and brought his face close to her stomach before inhaling deeply. "You don't appear to be fertile at the moment."

Breanna's mouth fell open. "You can tell that just by smelling me?"

He shrugged. "It's not one hundred percent, but it's pretty accurate, especially the closer you get to ovulation. When we're ready to have cubs…babies…it should be easy to conceive."

Part of her tingled with excitement at the thought of bearing his children, but she couldn't deny she was also fearful of the prospect. "Will our babies really be cubs? Will they be born looking like bears?" That was too much for her to accept, let alone embrace.

He shook his head again. "No, the shifter gene doesn't usually kick in until puberty, when it goes from dormant to active. In the meantime, our kids will appear to be as human as you are. They'll still have certain bear characteristics, of course, but the actual ability to shift won't be there from the start. It comes later."

"That's somewhat reassuring. I couldn't imagine breast-feeding if they had little bear teeth." He laughed along with her, and she relaxed in his arms. There was still a lot to work out, and she had to learn more about him, but as he lifted and carried her to the bed before joining her in it, she was certain she was where she was supposed to be. Wrapped in Rafe's arms, as she drifted off to sleep, she had no doubt he was her mate.

***

Sometime in the middle of the night, she woke with music thundering in her head. He was still asleep, so she slipped out of bed in search of anything she could use to record the notes darting through her brain. She often composed music mentally, but it never came this easily, and she never wrote it down. There had been no reason to do so.

After her parents had deemed her musical talent a waste, since she had no intention of using it publicly, she had kept it locked away inside herself. She hadn't touched a piano in four years, but her fingers itched to do so now.

She couldn't believe her luck when she entered his den and saw a small electric keyboard on one of the shelves. It was no baby grand, but it would do.

Breanna was even more delighted to learn it had a record function, and she pressed it before she began to play. The song flowed from her easily, as though each note was inserting itself into her mental sheet music before her fingers could play it.

It was a beautiful piece, with haunting moments, highlighted by happier notes. She didn't have a title for it, and it might never see the light of day, but when the music had ceased to flow through her, she was satisfied with what she had produced. Considering she hadn't played in four years, and she hadn't composed music other than in her brain for even longer, the sated, pleasantly exhausted feeling sweeping over her was a welcome sensation.

Rafe had given her back the music. Her new outlook and hope for the future had restored her ability to play. She would never fill concert halls, because she was too shy to be confident in front of crowds, but she could play.

She could have always played, but her parents had stifled that when she hadn't used her gifts the way they had deemed appropriate. Her cherished dream of being a piano teacher had been insignificant to the Dawsons, and she had let them steal it from her.

That realization left her sad. How could she have been so meek? New freedom swelled in her, reinforcing the determination that she had made the right choice fleeing from her parents' household and her arranged marriage to William.

Empty of the music that had flowed through her brain until she had woken to free it, she returned to the bed and curled against Rafe, pleasantly sated in more than one way. The emotional bliss of finding her music again almost rivaled the physical bliss Rafe's lovemaking inspired.

S I X

I took eight days for the snow to stop falling, and she spent those days falling ever deeper in love with her mate. They filled the time with loving, but also a lot of talking. She learned about his life as CEO of a small tech firm in Seattle, and she shared some details of her life, though she omitted the broken engagement. It was wrong to hide it, but she was embarrassed by how she had handled the situation.

The more they learned about each other, the closer they became.

The evening of the eighth day, they were wrapped in a comforter in front of the living room fireplace, trading kisses as they shared a bottle of wine. She leaned closer to Rafe, putting her head on his shoulder. "I could get used to this life," she said with a happy sigh.

She snuggled closer. "It's so different from my life in California, but that's a good thing. It has none of the fake bullshit the people there feel like they have to project, and I'm not pressured to conform, to lose weight, and to be perfect all the time. Living here in your cabin is pretty amazing."

Rafe wrapped his arm around her waist, pulling her closer. "It is amazing here, and I come during the winter months since it's the closest thing to hibernation I can find. It's not practical for the CEO of a company just take off and sleep for ten weeks out of the year."

She laughed softly. "No, I suppose it isn't. It would be hard to maintain your company that way." Breanna tipped her head sideways, so she could see his face better. "How does that work? Do you do everything from your computer?"

"Mostly. In the fifteen years I've been coming here to the cabin, I've rarely had to return to Seattle before my pseudo-hibernation is over. It's happened a few times, and when it does someone usually sends the company helicopter for me. I can be back in the city within two hours if I absolutely have to be. Otherwise, I enjoy the solitude and the winter snow, embracing my bear nature in a way I can't while living in the city. It's stifling there sometimes."

She nodded. "Like you're barely breathing, but you don't realize you're being suffocated until you get away from it and can take a deep breath." Her words were a metaphor, but not just for his situation. They were spot-on for the life she had left behind in California.

Breanna hadn't realized just how stifling it had been to live with her parents and always try to win their approval until she had fled and given up the attempt. It was liberating to no longer have to worry so much about how she looked, how she thought, how she spoke, or what she did.

There wasn't anyone from her old life that she really missed aside from Lupita. How pathetic was that? She had spent so long trying to win the approval of the people who'd given her life, and now she was relieved to be away from them instead of missing them. It was like she had wasted the last twenty-four years. A small shudder ran through her at the thought, and she suppressed the urge to cry.

Perhaps his bear senses allowed him to tune in to her emotions, because he seemed to realize she had entered a sad state. His hand was soothing on her back, and his embrace was comforting without being sexual. "What's wrong, sweetheart?"

She sniffed a couple of times and swallowed thickly before she could answer, determined not to cry. "I guess I just realized how much of my life I wasted trying to please people who are never going to be happy with me. I love my parents, but I don't think they feel the same way. I could never make them happy, even with my music. I don't know why I've tried for so long. I guess I'm just pathetic."

He growled softly, he and his bear clearly not liking her words. In one smooth motion, he flipped her so she sat on his lap, his hands cupping her face so she couldn't look away from him. "You aren't pathetic. Just the sexiest, most amazing woman I've ever met, and you're my mate. Everything that's happened to you and me has happened to bring us to this point. We can't change the past, but we can embrace the future."

Her lips trembled, and this time the tears she wanted to cry came from happiness rather than sadness. Determined not to let them fall either, she sniffed a couple of times again before leaning forward to kiss him slowly. "We do have a future, don't we?" she asked as she pulled away slightly.

"We have whatever kind of future you want, Breanna. If you don't want to go back to the city, we'll stay here forever. I have enough money that we can have this life, and I could walk away from the company."

She shook her head, her chest tight at the thought. "No, I wouldn't do that to you. I definitely like your cabin, and I can certainly envision spending weeks here at a time, but you're not giving up your dream for me. I know what that's like, and I won't let you do that."

His eyes were soft, and he kissed her again gently before speaking once more. "The company isn't exactly my dream. It was my dad's, and I'm just running it since he's retired. I enjoy it, but it isn't something I'm passionate about." His eyes shadowed. "Which dream did you give up and for whom?" There was an underlying growl in his words, and he was clearly angry at the thought of someone forcing her to do that.

She hesitated, wondering for a moment if it would color his opinion of her parents should they ever meet. Then she decided it didn't matter, because her parents were capable of making their own bad impression, just as he was capable of determining what they were like all on his own. He was too strong to let her influence him.

"I was an average child, just like I'm an average adult. I made okay grades, but I didn't stand out. The only area where I have any real talent is with music. I've been playing the piano since I was little, and I could pick up a tune without any training.

"My parents lavished lessons on me to prepare me for Juilliard and a career in music. I learned a lot in the two years they let me stay at Juilliard, including the fact I would never be able to perform in concert halls. Stage fright paralyzes me, and the music won't come when I'm facing others. Small groups are fine, but I could never do large concerts."

He scowled. "So? That doesn't mean you can't use music in other ways."

She nodded, wholeheartedly agreeing, though her parents didn't. "To their way of thinking, that was another failure, so they forced me to drop out of Juilliard. I could have stayed and try to go it alone, but I had no way to pay for it. Student loans wouldn't even begin to cover the tuition, and what would be the point? I'd end up doing something behind-the-scenes and probably with low pay, so why did I need a degree from Juilliard for that?"

He bared his teeth slightly, clearly grinding them to keep in angry words—words directed at her parents that she imagined would be fitting. As soon as she stroked his shoulder, his agitation eased, though his eyes remained shadowed. "I'm sorry. You had the right to finish school and do whatever you wanted with your life."

Breanna managed a small smile. "Oh, I finished college. They would be terribly ashamed of a dropout, but to punish me for my weakness, they sent me to state college instead. I actually liked UCLA, and that's where I met my friend Grace. Now I have a useless degree in music that I don't use, parents who will never approve of me, and a directionless future until I met you. Somehow, none of that matters now that I have you."

"I'm happy to hear that, but you should find a way to use your music when we return to the city, if that's what you want to do." They kissed again, this time not as gently. His mouth moved over hers, tongue sweeping inside to plumb the depths of her mouth. She met each stroke of his with her own tongue, determined not to be a passive participant.

Because they were naked under the comforter, a side effect of previous lovemaking, it required little effort to wiggle down his lap, pushing on his shoulders in the process. He laid down on the carpet, his stomach muscles contracting under her palm as she steadied herself to bring her mouth near his erection. She had yet to taste him, and she worried she wouldn't be very good at it. Her previous attempts with other partners had been lackluster, and the inconsiderate men she had been with hadn't hesitated to tell her.

Forcing herself to proceed, she bolstered her courage and wrapped her mouth around his shaft. He would like whatever she did to him, she reminded himself. He had so far. He seemed just as enamored with her and her body as he had the first day they had made love. He seemed to want her forever, so even if she performed an inadequate blowjob, she would have plenty of time to hone her skills.

Fortunately, passion kicked in, and her own need easily swept away the voice of doubt inside her mind that always held her back. For the first time ever, she enjoyed giving her lover oral pleasure as she tightened her mouth and bobbed up and down on him, gently massaging his testicles with her fingers as he groaned and grunted. It didn't take long before she could feel him trembling on the edge of release, and he sat up abruptly.

The rough side of him came out to play, and he rolled her over until she was on her stomach. Breanna let out a little yelp, but it was one of excitement instead of fear as he grasped her hips and lifted her buttocks into the air. A second later, his cock slid inside her heated folds, and her sheath contracted tightly around him. She was accustomed his size now, and both rough and gentle possession from him, depending on his need level, so her body welcomed her mate easily.

He held her hips in a hard grasp as he pushed in and out of her, his frantic urgency feeding hers and fueling her own arousal. She clutched handfuls of the comforter, using it as a makeshift pillow to steady herself as she arched backward in an attempt to match his deep, rapid thrusts.

They were making love fast and frantically, but each stroke of his erection in and out of her provided the perfect stimulation against her clit, and she came seconds before he did, letting out a small cry of release that his bellow of satisfaction blotted out.

She giggled into the comforter, unable to believe how much she loved the rough, bear-influenced side of him. He could be smooth and sophisticated, sweet and tender, or rugged and wild. He was the perfect combination of everything she could ever want or need in a mate.

To think she had nearly settled for something that was a pale imitation, that she had almost married William to please her parents, made her stomach churn with nausea. Even if she had never questioned her decision before— which she had for months—there was no way she could ever go through with such a match after seeing how love should be.

***

Sounds of helicopter blades woke them early the next morning. The sun was barely over the horizon when the *whomp, whomp, whomp* of the engine grew closer and closer. Rafe was immediately alert, jumping from the couch where they had ended up sleeping, too tired to go farther after hours of lovemaking.

She followed a moment later, stifling a yawn. Having looked forward to sleeping in, the interruption of the helicopter was unwelcome, even if it meant she could get back to civilization. Her heart dropped at the thought, because she had no desire to go anywhere away from Rafe or his cabin.

"I wonder what they need you for?" she asked as she wrapped the comforter around her and followed Rafe to the door.

He had paused briefly to shrug on jeans and his coat before shoving his feet into boots. "I don't know, but it's unusual for them to just show up without emailing or calling first."

She chuckled softly. "I'm not sure cell service has been restored, and you have to admit we've been pretty busy. Too busy to check email or even hear the *ping* notifying us of a new message."

He chuckled as well before his amusement turn to grimace. "They'd better not expect me to go back to the city, no matter how urgent the issue. There's no way I'm tearing myself away from you right now."

Her heart leapt with joy, and she knew whether or not Rafe went, she would be at his side. If she caught a ride on the helicopter back to Seattle with him, she wouldn't be going any farther than his home.

She hadn't yet told him she loved him, and he hadn't uttered the words either. It felt too new and fragile, perhaps even a little crazy, to be falling in love so early in their relationship, so she held back. She hoped his reasons were similar, rather than he was doubting his bear's insistence she was his mate.

All relationship speculation fled as they stepped out onto the porch in time to see the helicopter door opening. She let out a sharp gasp of shock at the sight of William dropping into the snow, his feet encased in snow boots. He walked jerkily through the snow with the same lack of grace she usually displayed, also unaccustomed to deep drifts of snow.

Unlike her, William was a god on the slopes, so it was amusing to see him struggle through several feet of snow to reach the cabin. He clomped up the stairs, his boots landing heavily as he kicked off the accumulated dusting.

He looked prepared for the Arctic rather than northern Idaho when he pushed back his thick fur-lined parka hood, his cold gaze settling directly on her. He seemed to disregard Rafe entirely. "What the hell are you playing at, Breanna? I don't have time for these idiotic games. It's taken days to track you down, and I'm fed up with this nonsense."

She could feel Rafe's tension radiating from him in waves, and a low growl came from the back of his throat.

She put a hand on his shoulder to soothe him, and as always, the bear inside responded just as well as the man to the calming effect. He fell quiet, though his posture was no less rigid.

She took a step forward, bringing herself just in front of Rafe. Firming her shoulders and tipping her chin upward, she forced herself to meet the frigid gaze of the man she had almost married. "I'm not playing any games, and you would know that if you read my email. I'm not going to marry you, William." She winced at Rafe's slight intake of breath behind her, followed by another growl as she took an additional step forward.

William scowled. "You most certainly are. Your father and I had a deal, and everything is ready to go. I will not allow you to humiliate me in this fashion. Do you have any idea what your father owes me? If I call in his debts, he'll be ruined, so get your fat ass on the helicopter and keep that mouth shut until I tell you to open it."

Before she could stop herself, Breanna lifted her arm and slapped him across the face. Then she clapped the same hand over her mouth as her other hand struggled to hold the comforter in place to maintain a modicum of dignity. She'd never struck someone before, nor had she ever been angry enough to do so. She didn't know whether to be giddy or throw up in response to her own actions.

She regarded him with a mixture of horror and the inappropriate urge to giggle as he cupped his face. The urge to laugh faded as his cold expression morphed to one of true anger. He lifted his arm, and for a moment she thought he was going to slap her back. Rafe must have thought the same thing, because he surged forward to move her from the path of a blow and pushed her behind him.

Instead, William waved his hand, and the helicopter door opened again. Two large men in suits paired with snow boots hopped from the chopper. They strode confidently through the snow, clearly more at ease in the terrain than she or William would ever be. In seconds, his henchmen flanked him, and her eyes widened when their hands went to their hips to reveal sidearms.

"Get her on the helicopter in one piece. If he gives you any trouble, do what you must. I have enough money to hide the death of some hillbilly cabin dweller."

One of the goons wrapped his hand around her upper arm, and in the process, the comforter slipped to reveal most of her upper body. As she hurriedly grabbed the fabric to cover herself, William sneered, increasing her anger. If he'd been within range, she would have slapped him again.

It was clear he didn't consider her good enough for him, but it was the other way around. He was an unworthy piece of crap, and having seen how a man should love her, she couldn't or wouldn't settle for less. "I'm not marrying you under any circumstances. I don't care if you ruin my father or level the entire West coast. There's nothing you can do to make me go along with that. I don't love you."

He paused in his retreat to the helicopter, turning back to face her as he snickered. "And you think I love you? You're nothing to me except a means to an end. I need your name and your family connections, and nothing more. After you pop out a couple of kids to anchor me to your social circles, I don't care what you do.

"You can come shack up with your hillbilly then if you'd like, but in the meantime, you're going back to California, you're going to marry me, and you won't say one word against me, or you'll regret it." He flexed his fist in a threatening manner as he uttered the last words.

What happened next happened so quickly she could barely follow the events. One moment, Rafe was beside her. The next, with a tearing of fabric, his bear was there instead. With a ferocious roar, Rafe batted aside the goon who had been holding a gun on him before turning to the henchman holding Breanna. Another swipe of his claws, and that man fell to the porch, unconscious as well.

William had stood frozen for a moment, clearly unable to comprehend what he was seeing. As Rafe turned toward him, he let out a bleat of terror and turned to run for the helicopter. It clearly took no effort at all for her lover to catch up with her ex-fiancé. He lifted William off his feet and forced the other man around to face him.

In the process, Rafe became himself again, though his claws still extended from his fingers. He held one threateningly near William's eye, not quite touching him, but making it clear he could easily kill the other man.

"Get your men and get off my property. Stay away for my mate, or you'll be the one who's sorry. Don't come back, or I'll deal with you in such a way you won't be able to leave again. Nod if you understand me." The command in his tone carried easily to Breanna, though she was a few feet behind them.

William nodded frantically, wincing when his own actions raked his skin against the tip of Rafe's claw. "What…what are you?" he asked in a high-pitched squeak.

"Just someone who wants to be left alone, and I want the same for Breanna. Go back to your life and forget about her, and we'll all be happy. Got it?"

William nodded again, almost as rapidly as he had before, but with more consideration for where Rafe's claw rested.

After a moment, Rafe lifted him off his feet and then dropped him, forcing the other man to land solidly on his ass in the snow. As William got clumsily to his feet, trying to stumble toward the helicopter, Rafe went to the goons.

He grabbed the first one by the back of his suit jacket and dragged his body off the porch, tossing him toward William. The men collided, forcing William back to his butt, and the other man landed on the snow with a small groan. Rafe repeated the move with the second one, this time not hitting William, who'd had the sense to stay down. "Don't forget to take your trash with you."

Breanna stood slightly behind Rafe, mainly because he wouldn't let her walk around his side, and watched William take off again in his helicopter with his henchmen a few minutes later.

"Thank you." She pressed a kiss to his shoulder as the helicopter gained altitude and veered away from them. "Do you think he'll be back? Will he tell people about you?"
Rafe was still tense, and he shook his head just once. "Who would believe him?"

She nodded, seeing his point of view. After William had nearly peed himself from fear, she couldn't imagine he would be back soon, if ever, since he was clearly unwilling to face Rafe again.

She pressed another kiss to his shoulder, surprised to find he was still tense. "They're gone."

He shrugged. "Yeah, they're gone. I just wish you'd told me them showing up might be a possibility to start with. I guess you forgot to mention you had been engaged?"

Slowly, Breanna stepped around him, ensuring their gazes met before she spoke. She trembled with cold and wrapped the comforter tighter around her. He was definitely upset, because he didn't notice or insist she get inside first before they spoke. "I was afraid to tell you. I'm not engaged to him any longer, and I haven't been since before I got here. Like a coward, I broke up with him via email, and I just ran away from everything. I'm sorry I didn't tell you the full truth, but I was embarrassed by my behavior. I promise I won't do that again."

Slowly, his tension faded, and abruptly he drew her against him as he dragged her back inside, seating her on the floor near the fire. "You need to warm up." He kicked off his boots and the remnants of his jeans before he joined her under the comforter, wrapping his arms around her again.

Their shared body heat, coupled with the warmth of the fire, soon chased away the last of the shudders and chills from both of them. She lay against him, content in the moment and assured he had forgiven her lapse of judgment. She shouldn't have lied to him, even by omission, but he seemed to understand she regretted it.

"There has to be complete honesty between us. Do you agree?"

She lifted her head from his chest to nod her agreement with this question. "Yes, I agree. Like I said, I'll never lie to you again."

He smiled softly. "And I'll never lie to you either."

"Thank you." She moved closer to her mate, laying her head on his shoulder again. "I love you, Rafe."

He growled, a sound of satisfaction. She stroked his chest, visualizing in her mind's eye rubbing his belly as she had when he had presented himself in bear form. He was rough and rugged, but inside, her Rafe was a marshmallow at heart.

He confirmed that when he said, "I love you, too. I waited thirty years for a mate I didn't think really existed. I'm glad I was wrong."

Before kissing him, she teased, "I love a man who can admit when he's wrong."

SEVEN

Her phone rang in the middle of the afternoon, and it was the first time she'd heard it in days. She hadn't bothered to check it when the snow had cleared, feeling no urgent need to get anywhere. Planning to stay with Rafe, she exchanged Facebook messages with Grace to catch up with her friend. When she told her she wouldn't be able to make it up to Calgary as soon as she thought, Grace seemed to understand.

She still hoped to meet up with her in person again soon, but she no longer needed to fling herself on her friend's mercy to have a place to stay or a way to rebuild her life. Not since her new life had started, the one she was building with Rafe minute by minute.

But when her phone rang, she was unsurprised to see her mother's phone number, and she swiped the screen to unlock the phone with a deep breath to brace herself. It was no longer tempting to turn off the phone or ignore the calls. She would prefer to get the confrontation out of the way so she could move on completely. "Hello?"

"My god, what have you done?" asked Estelle shrilly on the other end of the line.

"I hope you're happy with your shenanigans, young lady," said Bernard, her father. Clearly, they were on speakerphone together.

"I wouldn't call them shenanigans, but I am happy for the first time in a long time. Thank you for asking," she said sweetly.

Her father cursed, and her mother wept for a long moment before either spoke again. "If you don't get back here and make this wedding happen, we'll be ruined. Do you understand me? The money is gone. All of it. We need William to maintain our lifestyle, and you were part of the deal. You must come home now."

She took a deep breath again, actually relishing the moment as she felt her own transformation from scared little girl to capable adult reach fruition. "That place doesn't feel like home, Father, and I'm not sure it ever really was. I'm not the daughter you wanted, which you have made abundantly clear. I'm sorry for the situation in which you find yourself, but it's not my responsibility to ensure you're bailed out. I refuse to marry someone I don't love. I would like to have you in my life, but I expect that's an unreasonable prospect."

Dead silence greeted her words, and then her father cursed again. He rarely cursed in her or any woman's presence, bound by an old-fashioned code of behavior that forbade such things. To hear the curse words flow from his mouth was a shocking experience, though it only added to her urge to giggle.

She didn't know why she was so giddy, since it was a serious moment in a horrible confrontation between herself and her parents. Perhaps it was hysteria, or maybe it was just the rush of standing up for herself, which was quite liberating.

"Get back here right now. Enough of this nonsense."

She continued as if her father hadn't issued an edict. "If you and Mother decide you would like to be part of my life, I'll be happy to introduce you to my mate, a man I actually love. You might even approve of him, Father. He is a CEO, after all." *And a bear shifter*, she added silently as she stifled a giggle. There was no way her father would approve of that part. "I don't know if or when we'll get married, but if we do, should I send you an invitation?"

Her mother's hysterical cry and her father's shout of anger were the last things she heard before she disconnected the line. They had time to think about what they wanted, and she was surprisingly okay with it if they made the decision to cut her from their life.

It was what she expected, and it didn't hurt as much as it might have even two weeks ago, probably because they had cut her out long ago. She was simply finding the strength to let them go, and it wasn't a huge loss.

She was more mournful over losing the family she'd always wanted rather than the family she'd actually had. As Rafe came up behind her, nuzzling her neck while he wrapped his arms around her, she settled back against him happily. She was content with the family she was building, the family that would replace the lackluster one she'd had before. With Rafe at her side, how could she be anything but happy, knowing she was his mate? After all, bears mated for life, and she was a human who mated for life, too.

BONUS EXCERPT:
POLAR BOND

As she seated herself at the table, the first thing Grace noticed was the bewildering array of silverware choices. It was far different from her typical life in Calgary, where each meal came with a single fork, knife, and spoon. She knew Breanna had grown up in this world, so her friend seemed completely at ease with the silverware when she sneaked a peek at the bride and groom farther down the table.

Unlike the bride-to-be, Grace had grown up with humbler roots, more middle-class comfortable than old money wealthy. If it hadn't been for Breanna's parents being such judgmental jerks, she supposed she never would have met her best friend. They had considered it a punishment to send their daughter to state university—whereas Grace had considered it a privilege to attend UCLA, especially on scholarship—but their prejudices had created the perfect situation for the two girls who started as roommates to become best friends.

Which was what brought her to this table now, staring at the silverware. A glance to her right revealed an older woman selecting a fork from the outside for the salad, so she did the same.

A second later, all thoughts of silverware or anything else left her mind as the empty seat beside hers was filled. She glanced up, way up, to see who the late arrival was. She knew he had to be the best man, Kingston Meade, but they hadn't met yet. According to Rafe, he was in the middle of a merger that took a lot of time and attention.

"Sorry I'm late, old buddy, but it took forever to get Yamato to stop yammering," he said to the groom.

The new arrival was handsome. Handsome didn't even begin to cover it really. He had fine, sculpted cheekbones, pale gray eyes, and platinum-blonde hair styled in careless waves around his face. With broad shoulders that filled out his gray evening jacket in a mouthwatering fashion, she couldn't help imagining what she would find under that outfit, were her hands at liberty to discover for themselves. That thought, entirely inappropriate, caused her panties to grow damp.

Suddenly, the best man stiffened, his nostrils flaring as his head turned toward her. He didn't speak for a moment, his pale gray eyes somehow darkening slightly, looking more intense. There was a hint of watchfulness about him, almost like a predator sensing prey. No, that didn't seem quite right either. It was an indefinable quality, something with which she was unfamiliar, but for some reason, increased her arousal and made her nipples crinkle against the cream-colored sweater dress. She was thankful for the thick cable pattern that hid her reaction.

A moment later, he blinked, and the intensity was gone. He gave her a charming smile and held out a hand. "I don't think we've met. You must be Grace?"

She nodded, taking his hand and feeling clumsy as she did so. "Yes, I'm Grace DiPlaski. You must be Kingston?"

Instead of just shaking her hand, he did something unexpected. He turned it over and brought it to his mouth, pressing his lips lightly to her knuckles before returning her hand to her. "Yes. I'll admit I've been dreading the amount of time this wedding would require, and it's not even my own, but it's suddenly seeming a lot more fun. It's my understanding we get to spend a lot of time together."

She resisted the urge to giggle like an infatuated teenager, because she wasn't a teenager. The infatuated part wasn't far off the mark, she had to concede. Somehow, she sounded confident and airy when she replied, "I think it's one of the perks of the jobs."

"I'm sure your boyfriend or husband will miss your time though." It was a statement, not a question, but he was watching her closely as he sipped the white wine accompanying the first course at the rehearsal dinner.

She shook her head, feeling not even a twinge of regret that she had broken up with her longtime boyfriend just weeks ago. Before this minute, she had wished they had managed to make it past the wedding, so she'd have a plus-one for the event, not because she missed anything about her boring, stuffy ex-boyfriend. Now, she was relieved not to have a plus-one, though common sense dictated Kingston was only being polite, or perhaps indulging in a bit of lighthearted flirtation that would probably go nowhere.

Grace was pretty, and she knew it. With thick brown hair that curled riotously around her head without careful maintenance, honey-bronzed skin that was her natural complexion without foundation, and brown eyes, she got her fair share of second (and third) looks.

She was also curvy. Excessively curvy, by many standards. It didn't bother her that her clothes came from the plus-size department, because she loved her hourglass figure. A lot of guys appreciated it too, but in her experience, not the type like Kingston Meade.

He was a powerful businessman, the CEO of his company according to Rafe, and far more likely to date the typical standard of beauty, like a supermodel or an actress. She would have been a superstar during the Renaissance, but she was very much outside the conventional norms of beauty for today.

Of course, she might be wrong, she conceded, as she glanced at him from the side of her eye and caught his gaze resting blatantly on the swell of her curvy breasts, pressing against the cashmere fabric. The dress had been an expensive indulgence, one that had taken a good part of her monthly salary as a records clerk at Calgary Registry Services, but she couldn't regret having splurged on it with the way his eyes couldn't seem to tear away from her curves. It was the exact reaction she had been looking for when she had tried on the dress and plunked down her credit card with a small gulp.

"No, I don't have a boyfriend to worry about monopolizing my time. I assume your wife or girlfriend must be feeling somewhat resentful your responsibilities to the wedding, coupled with your merger?"

He took a moment to finish chewing the bite of Caesar salad, clearly relishing the anchovy melting in his mouth. "I don't have a wife or girlfriend."

"Boyfriend, perhaps?" she asked, carefully probing for information.

He shook his head. "Not one of those either, and I'm not in the market. To be honest, finding a mate was last thing on my mind...until recently."

Mate seemed like an odd word, but she supposed it fit. It always made her think of animals, like wolves or bears, mating for life. In some ways, it was a deeper-sounding commitment than marriage, which could end on a whim. Deciding she rather liked the term, she asked, "What changed your mind?"

"Love is in the air," he said with a hint of sarcasm alleviated by his playful wink. His gaze darted to Rafe and Breanna, who were busy feeding each other bites off their plates, though they had the same meals, and seemed oblivious to the people around them.

"No kidding. They're almost sickening, aren't they?" She didn't really mean that, of course. In fact, Grace was envious of their happiness. She certainly didn't begrudge Breanna having found someone she wanted to marry and spend her life with, but it underscored Grace's own loneliness.

Peter had been a fine substitute for a real relationship, and at times, he had been preferable to being alone, but she'd always known she wouldn't end up with him. There wasn't enough of a spark between them, and he was also kind of an asshole.

He had hidden that in the beginning, but it became more obvious as time progressed. She was happier alone now than she had been with him, but that didn't mean she wanted to embrace a life of solitude, and certainly not celibacy. "It must be nice," she said with a soft sigh.

"And kind of scary, to want someone so much, to need that person to the extent that your own happiness is all twined up with theirs. If something happens to them, you know you'll be miserable for the rest of your life. Sounds kind of frightening to want someone that much."

She arched a brow. "When you put it like that, I guess there is a strong component of fear, but that doesn't make me want it any less."

"Me either," he said, his voice rich with a hint of envy of his own.

The conversation changed to more lighthearted topics, and they became better acquainted as the meal progressed. By the time strawberry shortcake dishes, left in various states of completion, were whisked from the table, she was pleasantly relaxed, both from the food and his company.

There was a strong hint of awareness though, so she couldn't completely relax. It was as though they were attuned to each other, and her body buzzed just being near him. She couldn't imagine what it would feel like to have him actually touch her, but she sure wanted to know.

A few moments later, the band started playing a waltz, and he held out his hand. "Shall we?"

"Don't be silly," said a sharp voice from behind them. "It's kind of you to invite her to dance, Kingston, but I imagine a big girl like her would feel awkward on the dance floor."

Grace flinched at the words, uttered from such a bitchy mouth. Turning her head, she identified the source as a tall, slinky woman, who probably wore a negative dress size. There was something feline about her, perhaps in the way she moved, or maybe it was the way she purred Kingston's name. She seemed like a cat about to pounce on a disabled mouse.

Grace had never even spoken to the woman, and she had no idea who she was, but she wasn't a mouse. Whatever the reason for the woman's rude comment, she wasn't going to let it stand. Without speaking to the other woman, she turned her attention back to Kingston and extended her hand. "I'd love to." She couldn't deny a surge of satisfaction at the other woman's disgruntled expression when they walked past her, still hand-in-hand, and moved to the dance floor.

Held securely in his arms, closer than propriety dictated, she wasn't going to complain.

"I apologize for Ashley. She can be quite caustic at times. She's an old family friend, so I'm kind of stuck with her."

She followed his lead easily, thankful her mother had insisted on four years of ballroom dancing when Grace would have preferred jazz and tap. She was confident in her moves, easily matching his rhythm, as her body curled into his. Her soft curves nestled against the firm planes of his body, and her nipples hardened further. New wetness flooded her sodden panties as they pressed together, moving through the waltz with ease. "That's okay. Unless you raised her, I doubt you're to blame for her lack of manners."

He shuddered. "That would be a thankless task. I sort of pity her parents, but they overindulged her. She was an only child."

"So is Breanna, but her parents certainly didn't overindulge her."

Kingston nodded, his expression bordering on sad. "She told me a little bit about growing up in the Dawson household. Sounds like it was rough."

"Yes, it does." When she had first met Breanna, she had envied the other woman's wealth and seeming ease of acquiring anything she needed in life.

It hadn't taken long to get better acquainted with her shy roommate and realize that while her parents had everything money could buy, they were stingy with doling it out to their daughter unless she lived up to their unreasonable expectations. They were even more miserly with love and affection. Once or twice, Grace had tried to gently suggest that Breanna not worry so much about what her parents thought, but it had seemed to upset her roommate, so she'd avoided the subject.

Things had certainly changed since Breanna met Rafe. Her best friend was now a confident woman, held firmly in her soon-to-be husband's embrace.

Kingston was holding her just as firmly, she realized, and each deep breath she took pressed her breasts against his chest and further sensitized her nipples. She had the mad urge to tear open his dress shirt, rip off his tie, and press her sweater-covered breasts against his bare chest. Thankfully, it was a passing fancy, and she had it under control before she could even so much as reach for the first button on his pearl-gray shirt.

When the music ended, she started to step back, but his arms tightened again, pulling her even closer. It was an unsubtle hint that he wasn't done with her, but that was fine, because she wasn't done with him either.

It had been a long time, if ever, that she had spent the night dancing in her lover's arms. Kingston wasn't her lover, but she didn't think she was completely crazy to entertain the idea that he would be at some point. Her best friend's wedding was the perfect opportunity to indulge in a harmless fling, though Grace wasn't really the fling type.

She'd never been able to sleep with someone she had just met, even if there was an intense attraction. Admittedly, she'd never been so attracted to someone so instantly before in her life. It went completely against her nature, but she couldn't guarantee she would turn him down if he bent her over the dessert table right now and feasted on her feminine essence. The thought made her whimper lightly, and her thigh muscles tightened involuntarily in reaction to the dart of arousal shooting through her core.

Kingston growled softly, an honest-to-goodness growl that was more animalistic than human. It was a sexy sound, albeit strange. She looked up at him, noticing again how tall he was compared to her. She was already on the short side, but he seemed like he had to be extremely tall, at least 6'4".

"Are you all right?" It was an inane question, and it wasn't what she really wanted to ask. Somehow, she bit back the urge to ask him if he wanted to slip away to the coat closet. Since it was April, there would probably still be some coats in there to hide their activities. Reminding herself she wasn't the exhibitionist type, any more than she was the type to hop into bed with a stranger, she bit back the urge.

"No," he said in a half-growl. That intense look was back again, the one that made her feel hunted, but not fearful of being caught. The idea of him chasing her down and taking her sent a thrill of dark pleasure through her rather than one of fear. "Is there something I can do to help?"

His body thrummed with energy, and he seemed to be on the verge of saying something deliciously wicked, but a cool splash down her back and side made her gasp and distracted her. Grace pulled away from him to find the source of discomfort, shocked to see red wine bleeding through the soft cashmere cream dress.

Stricken, she looked up to meet the cold eyes of Ashley, holding an empty wine glass. Her smirk of satisfaction fooled no one when she said, "Oh dear, how clumsy of me. Well, you must run along and clean up." Without glancing at Grace again, she turned to Kingston, neatly sliding her body into the space between them. She wrapped her arms around his neck and pressed her slender body to his. "It looks like you need a dance partner."

Grace had to resist the urge to grab a handful of the strange white hair of the woman who had just doused her very expensive dress with a very expensive Burgundy wine. From a distance, she had thought Ashley was another platinum-blonde, but up close, she could see her hair was actually white. It was strangely beautiful, and the woman herself was beautiful everywhere except her attitude.

With a small sigh of surrender, knowing she needed to get the dress off and tend to the stains as quickly as possible if she had any hope of saving the expensive garment, she turned away from them and rushed from the ballroom of the hotel hosting the reception dinner. The nearest ladies' room was right across the hall, and she ducked inside.

It wasn't ideal, but she would have to dab at the dress she wore before running up to her room. She would send it immediately down to be laundered, but she wasn't hopeful that the hotel could save it either. She had just gotten a handful of wet paper towels when the door opened, and her best friend slipped inside.

Breanna wore an expression of concern, and she crossed the bathroom quickly on high heels that tapped with every move. Her straight posture and confident pose was a stark contrast to the shy and timid woman she'd been before Rafe. "What happened?"

Grace shrugged. "To be honest, I'm not sure. I mean, I know what happened, but I don't know why." She quickly recounted for Breanna the story of how her dress became stained, along with the catty remark Ashley had made to her earlier before she started dancing with Kingston.

"She's jealous," said Breanna firmly. There wasn't a hint of doubt in her voice.

Grace laughed softly as she dabbed at the wine spots. Little specks of paper towel stuck to the white fabric, and she knew she was fighting a losing battle. "What? Why would she be jealous of me? Have you seen her? I mean she's a little strange-looking, with her pale skin and that white hair, but she's beautiful."

"She's leucistic. Kind of like a form of albinism," said Breanna.

Grace nodded. "I didn't know the term, but I thought it might be something like that. I wasn't sure though, since she doesn't have pink eyes like most albino animals."

"They should be bright green instead of that pale blue, because the girl is green with envy. It's no secret she wants Kingston, and she's always bugging him. There's the answer for you. She was jealous of the time he's spending with you. Clearly, she realizes he wants you, and she wants to make sure that doesn't happen."

Grace wanted to believe her friend, but she was assailed by an unexpected dart of self-doubt. It was the same one that had come to her earlier, reminding her men like him dated supermodels, not super-curvy girls. "I still don't think she has anything to worry about."

Breanna cocked her head slightly, sending caramel-brown waves fluttering down her shoulder. "Really? You're really going to stand there and pretend like we didn't need to have the fire department on standby with you two heating up the floor like that?"

Her cheeks flamed. "You're one to talk. You and Rafe were practically humping on the floor."

Breanna laughed, clearly not going to deny it. "The difference is, we're already mated—I mean engaged, and about to be married, so there's no reason to deny our attraction. The question is, my dear, why are you denying his for you and yours for him?"

"I'm not denying I'm attracted to him, but I just find it hard to believe I might be his type. I am a sexy piece, but I have a feeling guys like him go for girls like Ashley, not me."

Breanna snorted. "If that were the case, he could've gone for her night after night. The chick is not subtle. Don't worry about her, because he's clearly not interested in Ashley Toth. He's interested in Grace DiPlaski." With a firm nod, she glanced at the doorway. "I have to get back to the party. Are you all right?"

Grace nodded. "I will be. I'm going to slip up to my room and try to send this down to the laundry to see if they can salvage it." Thinking of the amount on her credit card, waiting to be paid off, she could have cried at the waste. Either that, or plucked every white hair out of Ashley's head.

"If you won't feel offended though, I'll probably just stay in for the rest of the night. I don't have another fancy outfit with me, aside from my dress for the wedding and what I'm wearing to the bachelorette party tomorrow night, and I'm just kind of drained after the whole Ashley Toth experience."

Breanna gave her a quick hug, careful to avoid the side splashed with red wine so as not to stain her own pale gold dress. "Of course, Grace. Just unwind and forget all about Ashley, but don't discount Kingston. I don't know him as well as I know Rafe, of course, but I think I know him well enough to tell when he's attracted to someone. He wants you."

"Well, let's see if he takes me." She winked at her friend as Breanna departed before spending another five futile minutes trying to wipe away the stains. With a sigh, she conceded defeat and tossed the paper towels into the trash can. After washing her hands and drying them with another round of paper towels, she walked to the door.

When she opened it, her heart leapt in her chest, and she pressed a hand to it as though to hold it in. "You startled me."

Kingston leaned against the doorway, a white robe held out to her. "Sorry. I was just waiting for you to come out. I had the hotel concierge secure this for you. I thought you might want to put it on and get out of that wet dress." His eyes moved to her breasts, where the splotch of wine had spread across her left side, making her bra and beaded nipple visible on that side.

"Thank you." She reached for the robe and started to slide it on over the dress, moved by his thoughtfulness almost as much as the lust she saw shining in his eyes. Breanna was right. He wanted her, and she wanted him.

It was an untenable position, simply because she wasn't certain about indulging in a temporary relationship. What else could it be, with him living in Seattle and her in Calgary? She'd be the first to admit her job as a records clerk wasn't exactly career material, and she wouldn't be opposed to relocating to Seattle for the right man, but she still didn't think the relationship would go anywhere besides the bedroom.

"Take off the dress first." That growl was back in his voice, and his eyes had darkened again.

She shivered under the gaze, surprised to find her hands moving to the hem of her dress. She wasn't really going to take off the garment standing in the open doorway of the ladies' bathroom, was she? She hesitated with her fingers at the hemline, staring at him uncertainly.

"Please, take it off. I want to see you."

Forgetting all about anyone who might come by, and already knowing she had the ladies' room to herself, at least for the moment, Grace obeyed his commands. She wasn't really the submissive type, but he was just so commanding, and that intense edge surrounding him made her want to do whatever he said. She pulled off the soggy dress and extended it to him to trade for the robe he had taken back. He held it carefully as he handed her the robe, his gaze not wavering from her body as she slipped on the terrycloth. She hadn't tied the tie yet when he spoke again.

"Take off your bra."

She stared at him, a new wave of uncertainty sweeping over her. Grace nibbled on her full lower lip as she hesitantly reached for the front clasp of the bra. It was one of her favorites, also a new purchase.

The creamy satin was light enough to be unnoticeable under the cream-colored dress, and it provided adequate support for her larger-than-average breasts, while still making her feel ultra-feminine with the pearl and bow accent, coupled with a flirty front clasp. Her hands shook slightly, with anticipation instead of anxiety, as she opened her bra, leaving the straps on her shoulders. Her breasts sprang free, and his deep inhale was gratifying to hear.

A millisecond later, the unwelcome sound of heels tapping on the marble floor penetrated through the haze of passion trying to overtake her. Quickly, she pulled the robe closed and tied the sash, completely covered by the time their unwanted visitor came into sight.

She wasn't surprised to see Ashley standing behind Kingston, a possessive hand dropping onto his bicep. "I wondered where you had disappeared to, darling?"

Kingston shrugged her off, but the hand came back immediately. "What are you doing here, Ashley? Have you come to apologize?"

Ashley giggled, an annoyingly high-pitched sounds. "Why should I apologize when she's the clumsy one who hit my arm?"

How the story had changed already. As Kingston called her on that, Grace took advantage of the moment to slip away quietly. She was in no mood to face down the other woman, and she wasn't certain she would get through it without ripping out a few hairs and perhaps marring that pretty face. Grace wasn't a scrapper by nature, but she could hold her own if she had to. She didn't want to end up with a black eye or something equally unfortunate for her friend's wedding pictures though.

Most of all, she escaped from Kingston and her own re-action. She wanted him with intensity that overrode common sense and her normal behavior. She had to think long and hard about if she could really handle a short-term affair. By the time she got to the point where she committed her body, her mind was already committed. It had been that way for her previous relationships, and though each had fizzled out or blown up spectacularly, depending on the circumstances, she had known her partners well at least in the beginning.

Maybe what she needed was something completely different. Maybe that's where she had gone wrong. Instead of trying to get to know her partners and connect with them beyond the physical level, maybe she should just surrender to her own biological imperative and jump on Kingston the next time the opportunity arose. She still hadn't decided on that as she fished the key card from her tiny evening purse and entered the room.

As she stepped inside, she let out a small groan of realization. Her dress was still in Kingston's hand, assuming Ashley hadn't torn it from him and ripped it into pieces in a snit. She should do something about retrieving it, but she was just too frazzled to face going back downstairs tonight. She didn't want to run into Ashley, and she still wasn't confident she could withstand Kingston's charms if she sought him out, even for something as innocuous as retrieving her dress.

Instead, she used her cell phone and texted Breanna to ask her to fetch the dress after the party was over. A hot shower restored some of her equanimity, along with removing the sticky wine feeling, and she slid between the sheets naked shortly thereafter. She had never enjoyed wearing nightgowns or pajamas, and now as an adult, she reveled in sleeping nude.

Despite her uncertainty and her exhaustion from the evening, she couldn't seem to turn off her mind as it insisted on spinning fantasies of Kingston in the bed with her, equally nude, their bodies pressed together. She could feel his hands on her in her imagination, and he would be silky smooth to the touch too, except where she ran into crisp chest hair, or perhaps the hair shielding his tender sac.

She could easily imagine wrapping her hands around his shaft, certain he would be large and well-endowed just judging by how big he was everywhere else. Her mouth watered at the thought of tasting him, and she whimpered as she pictured his head between her legs.

Her hand was a poor substitute for the imaginary tongue magic her phantom lover worked as she fantasized while stroking herself to climax. As she hovered on the edge of orgasm, Grace vowed she would shove aside her own reservations and seize the moment if there was another opportunity with Kingston. She hoped she hadn't made a mistake by walking away earlier, and that she wasn't headed toward an even bigger mistake by planning to jump in without looking.

With soul-shaking certainty, she knew she would be Kingston's lover before the wedding was over. The question remaining was: for how long?

ALSO BY ARIA CHASE

EMERALD CITY SHIFTERS

Polar Bond
The Bear's Secret Baby
One Night With A Bear
Fighting For Her Bear
Bought By A Bear

SUNDOWN WOLVES

Temptation
Reparation
Distraction

ABOUT THE AUTHOR

Paranormal romance author Aria Chase combines her fascination with the occult and her undying love for happily ever after to create steamy shifter reads that are perfect for devouring in one night.

Visit www.ariachase.com to connect with Aria via Facebook, Twitter or email.